The Botnet, the Glitch, and the Payload

SKELM.realm(001)

The SKELM Chronicles: Reprehensible Deeds of a Detestable Scoundrel

SKELM.crumb 1

Darby Skelm

SKELM.debug

Sana Abuleil & Maxine Meyer

Copyright

The Botnet, the Glitch, and the Payload: SKELM.realm(001)

© 2025 SKELM LLC. All rights reserved.

Published by THE ALIVE BUNCH

An imprint of SKELM LLC

ISBN: 978-1-968564-07-0

First Edition: August 2025

This is a work of fiction. Any resemblance to actual persons, living or dead, or actual events is purely coincidental. Any resemblance to corporations currently optimizing your reality is purely inevitable.

skelmcorps.com

Open mouths, empty heads, big bytes.

Dedication

For the incompatible.

तत्त्वमसिं

- Encrypted SKELM Proverb -

Contents

SKELM.quest 1

MOV boot.seq, AX ; The Invocation of Digital Muses

SKELM.trial 1

JMP init_odyssey.sh ;
User Autonomy Bypass

The eels writhe against my legs, their slick skins catching fractured light from the buzzing neon sign outside. I wake in a bathtub and immediately wish I hadn't. It's not the first time I've found myself in this situation, but it's the first time the bastards have almost found me too. I open my hazel eyes and curse the day I decided retinal implants were a good idea. They work better than I remember. I see it all at once: the crumbling tile, the stolen code chips, the fractured circuits. Even a rogue spec floating outside the door. Their latest debt collector drones. I'm soaked and alive and out of here before the neural-gel towels have time to dry. Once more with feeling.

I peel the first of the slimy creatures off me and toss it on the floor, scrambling to piece together what went wrong. Maybe I'm dead already, just another glitchy file uploaded to an abandoned archive. More eels and more years to go before I rest. But my brain and the wriggling nightmare are clear enough to know that they haven't caught me yet. Every waking thought floods in at once. Most of them boil down to the fact that I'm knee-deep in what passes for reality around here. If I'm still calling this place *here,* that is. Another squeeze and another coil slithers away, a gross tangle of scales and shiny new trauma. The last thing I remember is swiping into this slum motel somewhere on the fringes of an existence my old life wouldn't recognize. Surprised even me. A stolen feed suggested I was back in the genetic casserole of Iowa. Everything since then is as muddled as a collective consciousness prayer at a Church of Digital Gnosis funhouse.

I get to my feet, almost naked except for the eels. The wind from outside has a colder bite than I do. I knew this would happen eventually, but the Neural Sorcerer said I had weeks before they sent the dogs. He should have had the goddamn courtesy to say I'd be taking a bath. I hear the buzz outside the room, a dull hum against the chattering neon. Maybe I'm hallucinating and they've found me, years past due and strung out in a motel tub. Water crashes down like a VR cleanse session and washes the creatures and any remaining doubt onto the tile. Not enough credits for this simulation. Never enough credits for anything.

Everything is exactly where I left it. Scrambler, neural-gel towels, desperate bids for freedom. I've been here for a while, sitting like a soaked trophy waiting to be claimed. There's a flash from the corner of the room, some distant line of reality crossing mine. They must have tracked my coordinates back to a package I picked up in an expired software district, chased me to this time-lapsed crash site, and pinned me to my very last dot. I could sit back and let them take what's left. Clean slate. Blank mind. Roll my whole identity back to version 0.0. Or I can fight it. Because what the hell else am I supposed to do? My neural systems kick back online. Breathe deep. Process. Move.

First, the coders on the LED tell me it's a lock. Then they tell me it's chaos. I'm not one for dramatic gestures, but even a chimera-bait clown should know that an untraceable hijack doesn't get messy without a push. I haven't met a bad tip I didn't trust. Now look where it's got me. Desperate, underwater, in Iowa.

I'm halfway to the door when I see the full scope of it. More sub-drones than should ever make its way to a freelancer - certainly more than they could have spared for a dead account. They're more advanced than the last run-in, these DebtHound™ fuckers. They've upgraded since Chicago, bio-components and synthetic pheromones. They've gotten even better at sniffing out the suffering and credits they think are theirs. The first has to be a couple floors up, angling the swarms into place. I wish I had that monk here now to tell me how all this confusion is clarity. I'd throttle him with a stray robe. In two hours, the nothing I believe in will matter even less than it already doesn't. Just another time-stamped incident report. Or worse, an involuntary demo of their experimental drones.

They're persistent, I'll give them that. Almost as stubborn as me, Darby Skelm, zeroed-out freelancer and king of nothing at all. I rip a jagged tee shirt off the grimy floor and hear their chorus move in sync, assembling their song from broken fugues. I won't be a coda. I won't be next.

Spar with a bunch of DIY renegades for too long and suddenly your whole life becomes optional. Chimera left me for broke, nearly glitching into scraps. Even said so themselves. *We need your bones. We need your systems. We need your doubts*. Two days in and I already hear the bastard sons of RunTime asking how they ever got along without my strategic hopelessness.

The real debt is what we let it be. Don't tell the Digital Oligarchy. I wish those deep-Gnostic grifters half a mind - twice as loud, half as sound. Of course, they still come out ahead. Disciples don't owe what they haven't yet perceived, and their hierophant had the insight to call it an indeterminate venture, prophesied margins blurring all the way to zero. Just need to make it one month. One week. One half-life. Then something else distracts them, reality recycles itself, and the chips fall squarely on the prophet's self-fulfilling lap. I just didn't know how right they were about nothing mattering. No funds. No job. No trust.

I look through the half-open door and see what the consensus says. Hard to ignore. Even harder to believe. There's a drone swarm waiting for me. One glitch is all they need, and this time, my scramble feed isn't fast enough to seed a crash.

These rigs run deep, more debt and pursuit vectors than anything I've seen before. They're playing out of the Book of Advanced Collections. But I've got the entire Systems Log on my side. Just not on the side that makes any difference. Nothing left to hide behind except a couple junked IO relics and the growing suspicion that I shouldn't have ditched Mom's encrypted LinkedIn request. Some relevance might have saved my skin. The feed still rolls through the cracks of my implants, a litany of wasted context for a guy who can barely remember what it was like to keep this much junk stored in meatspace. Haven't felt that need in years. Mostly because I haven't felt at all. Then there's this morning, and it makes me feel alive in ways that scare what's left of me.

Giant towers of logic and compound statements reach for the sky. A luminescent fog rolls in, half the speed of an idle thought. Sub-drones run on hyper-coded tenacity, convergence tech and flash memory and living circuitry barely contained by their crystal-encased neural cores. They recompile their urgency. Get closer. Even their fucking anxiety gets closer. Real credit and virtual lives might be easy to erase, but this is as personal as an eviction notice written in blood and printed on what used to be your spleen.

Only gets worse if I die before they drag me back to solvency. First job that gets your rate and your whole goddamn history. All I know is that there's an arms race at stake. I run for cover with less grace than an uncompiled for-loop and wish the rest of me had half the freedom of my RAM. Maybe then I wouldn't remember how easily I walked into this. Three months pretending to be myself again. Three months thinking this job was going to change everything. Probably the reason it didn't change a thing.

If I pull this off, it'll be because even a hardline Oligarchy scout gets rattled. Also helps if he doesn't know the blueprint for the kind of salvage I can run on these odds. Maybe I'll get captured. Maybe they'll just laugh and wipe my caches clean and turn me into an electric ghost. All I know is that I'm not giving up until I'm the very last thing I have to let go of.

The last day it felt this dangerous, I was in love with existing.

Maybe that's the way it still is. Maybe I survive. I doubt it, but that's the difference between me and those cross-threaded corps and priests - and fuck you, Mrs. Skelm. It's what keeps me chasing my breath, coming up with something, fighting this digital beast for the smallest hope that I haven't yet. I hit the sequence with less coordination than I hit a target quota. Miracles don't matter, but somehow, I do. The kid of death and dumb luck, careening out into the garbled neon streets, rewriting my epilogue with every hurried breath.

SKELM.trial 2

CALL assemble_crew.py
; Behavioral Surveillance

Neon reflections chase me into the zeppelin's cargo bay. Industrial ghosts blink across augmented eyes as I get my first look at our newly stolen hideout. Syron, a stim-junkie demigod, ignores my entrance with deliberate intensity. She jabs at a malfunctioning terminal, sleeves rolled above circuitry tattoos and hands shaking with meaning. The vat-grown calamari projects squid-like calm, using way too many tentacles to sync control panels and sip a dirty martini. In one twitchy corner, the nihilist monk scribbles dogma onto data pads, his impenetrable Wingdings mixing ancient prophecy with stoner irony. The rest of the zeppelin clangs with black-market AI doing vocal warmups. "Let not thy stains linger," it says, sounding like Nietzsche in a 1950s radio ad. This giggle populates the air with other absurdities, and I have to wonder: *Is existential piracy always this cute?*

I stand like a lone pixel in a misrendered frame, surrounded by chaos that smells like overclocked solder and freshly generated despair. I glance at a series of pipes tracing the walls like robotic vines, all colors and dissonant frequencies. Strobing LEDs give the place a 4 a.m. murder-motel-in-Iowa glow. The air is thick with junk-shop karma, tangy as neural interface gel and twice as dangerous. Our newest headquarters look like something hacked from IO.wav and fueled on caffeine and debt.

Syron scowls at the terminal with an expression usually reserved for ex-lovers and 404 errors. She keys in a stream of angry code, glitch patterns playing across her oversized hoodie. "Someone here likes this mess," she mutters, side-eyeing me without breaking pace.

I wonder if "likes" is the right word for this digital commune of maladjusted genius. I don't plan to crew with Syron again, but the universe compiled us into the same hot mess of a heist, and here we are. The terminal flickers, briefly losing power like a junkie nodding off mid-rant. She smacks it, and the screen leaps back to life with the vigor of one who's been in this abusive relationship before.

"I'm touched you remember me," I say, studying the way her hands find focus amid chaos. *They're resourceful*, my hands say back. *Efficient*.

Syron rolls her eyes, tired and cutting. "My heart still works, even if it's written in deprecated code." She finishes one line and shifts to another project: raising a cigarette to her lips, exhaling timebombs in technicolor smoke. The kind of smoking gun you marry, if you're too broke to kill it.

I pretend not to care as much as I do, flicking my gaze to the calm amid this storm. The vat-grown calamari hovers like the most conspicuous surveillance drone, executing eight-point movements with something resembling grace. Its skin pulses in time with its thoughts, revealing circuitry veins and scrolling subroutines. In the cosmic soup of underground bio-engineering, it rises to the surface with all the clarity of a Craigslist missed connection.

It notices me noticing and adjusts the rhythm of its *tap-tap-tapping*, tentacles moving like interpretive dancers with Wi-Fi connections. "Hello, Darby," it says, as if those words have never been more than 56% true. "Our illustrious crew captain finally arrives."

"Late for the chaos as usual," Syron says, not even bothering to aim the jibe away from herself.

I throw a grin into the air and hope the right one catches it. "Time is an illusion. At least, that's what a talking squid once told me."

"Don't drag me into your temporal insecurities," it says, three tentacles sipping martini, four animating my neurotic life decisions on a shared display, and the last tickling a port as if it were capable of laughter. The martini's got two olives. It offers me one and saves the other for a potential apocalypse.

"Those kinda don't happen without me," I say, remembering how the calamari can bend bio-code and mental states, converting hackers into jelly with pure chill. "How long until we're live?"

It's too busy producing a tentacular sonnet to respond immediately. Two subroutines take bets on whether he's talking about the system or himself.

I want to bet, too. "Any chance you're wrong about us being right?"

"We've aligned our tentacles with favorable fates," it says, dipping metaphysical humor in cocktail sauce. "What is a reality hacker without ambition?"

"Or failure," Syron says. "Look at you two - sounds like Darby found a friend he won't screw." Her laughter rings across the cargo bay, knowing and edged.

I laugh back, something not unlike nostalgia sharpening my throat. It tastes metallic and strangely new. I glance toward the nihilist monk, suspended upside-down in meditative oblivion. His orange robes are 100% recycled piety, modded with cooling vents and USB ports. The monk claims to wander aimlessly, but his internal clock is synced to the decimal.

I swear the monk doesn't notice me, but somehow, the LED indicators on his shaved head blip welcome messages in binary. In the Neo-Mythic Datascape, where even blind faith is retina-enhanced, I figure anything's possible.

With pre-cognitive sarcasm, Syron says, "A hundred creds say Darby thinks he's found religion." I leave that bet for the monk to arbitrate.

The nihilist finishes a Wingdings manifesto, ending with an elegant shrug and a minor enlightenment. Symbols bloom from a terminal beside them, anciently absurd and pretentiously wise.

The monk gives me an ambiguous nod, because that's the only kind he has. This untangles the first few threads of my mind. "Nice to be aboard," I say, checking the translations of *nothing matters at all, and yet here you are, and all profits are ultimately transcendent.*

"Let not thy stains linger, for even filth finds absolution in truth," says the ghostly AI voice, filling my last doubts with cleansing absurdity. Syron waves a nonchalant hand at me as the rest of the zeppelin shudders to life. It drones with loose components and philosophical uncertainty. Wingdings. Tentacles. Static hearts. Like an armory built entirely of bright, shiny questions.

If this is what it means to steal a second chance, I figure we'll have plenty of bullets before long.

I plunge further into the zeppelin's digital warren. The AI's vintage chorus accompanies every step, while Syron's attention flits between me and a lit cigarette. She leaves her terminal with a soldier's speed, gesturing me toward the deck as though I'm a hostile mission objective. The calamari's display shifts in the digital equivalent of a magic-eye puzzle, haikus cycling through pixelated patterns. The monk continues to produce religious conviction at a speed that would frighten Gutenberg. Even the ship's walls hum with reality's vague outline, holographic projections shimmering into grotesque birth and decomposing back into code. I finally reach Syron, our eyes meeting with unreadable certainty. "It can't be that bad," I say.

She cracks a smile so thin it feels hand drawn. "Wait 'till we start." Together, we pace through this fractured neon womb of strange agendas and stubborn dreams.

My strides form the pacing heartbeat of the zeppelin's chaos, synchronicity occasionally glancing against me before veering off into tangents of their own. Drones bleep absurd harmonies while something buzzes in a wall like a trapped insect powered by quantum fuel. I remember this - disorder that forgets itself, reality improvising. I drink in the strange tempo like water from an emergency supply.

Syron makes good on the projection of her limbs, sprinting toward me before words catch up. She burns through the space, smoke pixels scattering in her wake. "You look better with egg on your face than you do waiting," she says, knowing exactly how that sounds like love to a fool.

The ash of her cigarette changes shape mid-air. It falls in parabolas, infinitely rare for someone who takes shortcuts so seriously. "Catch up, slowpoke," she says, with about the same amount of affection.

"I was getting the layout," I say, doing exactly as she instructs. The urgency of her movements leaves no room for even metaphysical doubt. Our reunion has no choice but to run.

The calamari executes simultaneous diagnostics on the variables of my intentions and the likelihood of success. Six variables twitch in code poetry, the remaining two holding mixed bets and drinks.

"Trying not to sink with the ship?" Syron says as I closes the distance.

I register twelve unfiltered hours of punk-nihilism and let go of the rest. "Sink is a state of mind."

"The softshell scans Darby's mind," Syron says to the monk. "Bet it thinks he's a shipwreck!"

She laughs the kind of laugh that loses as often as it wins. She knows I'm here for it and all the things I won't catch. It feels like an arrival even before I've made it past hello.

One calamari tentacle waves lazily in the general direction of optimism. A thousand percent probability.

I swear the AI switches to italics when it addresses me.

The floating surveillance squid offers reassurances. "We're taking water, not sinking." It cross-references with Synonym-Finder.exe, then says, “Never mind - "

"I got the message," I say. I've spent enough time on water, real or imagined, to recognize its absence. The calamari accepts my quick understanding with equanimity and the unerring skill of a pool shark.

Encrypted mantras display across the walls, swimming in my periphery. Most in elegant, even lines, with the occasional free verse catching light and shadow:

Mind

Like

A

River

Damns

Itself

<0>_____<1>_____<2>

"Not exactly helping," I joke.

The rest cycle like parables of neural-spliced postmodernism.

All outputs equal

Or error awaits input.

Choose not. Who are you?

<Yes>No<Yes>No<Yes>No<Yes>No>

Syron makes sure I see it. "Remind you of anyone?"

The colors shift as the ship parses intent. They flash in bug-zapper purples and reds, dragging the crewmates through glitchy purgatory.

I give them what they've asked for.

Nothing.

And something.

A time-share on the kind of ambiguity it takes digital wizards to unravel. I wonder how many tangles I'll see through. Whether the LED has compiled that part of the story.

The calamari remains non-committal, flashing plans in its chromatophoric script. "This way to a probably impossible fate," it says, colors smudging like ink when reality got too wet.

I accept the invitation. Reality's already a soggy and surprising roommate.

Further along, the monk produces impenetrable messages with relentless confidence, casting symbolic incantations into the neural storm. Some blink in frenetic red, glitched alarm beacons in existential emergency:

8°63<<88>>90

33<-☆ ★-44-★ ☆->22

But as I approach, the symbols rearrange themselves into perfect symmetry:

44-★ ★-44

64-64

It's reassuring to be misunderstood, I think. *It's where all the fun happens.*

The display updates itself as the ship sends new signals, the story written faster than we can live it. I decide it has already. And always has. And that it will again.

The walls strobe the messages of fate, willful accidents dancing like high-risk ghosts on a billionth marriage:

1 / 0 / 1 / 0

Better never than before.

0 / 1 / 0 / 1

More glowing squares hover above, broadcasting updates in shrines of geometric clarity. Some see me better than others. It's like all the times we've crewed together. I'm following signs, hoping for what comes next.

The calamari decides I'm worth believing in.

One of the floating lights shifts its message when I pass. "Heh," it says, as close to amused warmth as a self-defined universe can get.

I match symbols with memory, seeing a part of me I've spent with everyone.

"Cleanse thy circuits and iron thy doubts," the AI says, skipping more seriously than before. The crew will go mad. Or brilliant. Or find out if they can be both. I think they're pretty good odds.

Finally, I meet Syron's reckless certainty as she paces like a general in enemy time zones.

She softens slightly, humanity and existential armor thinning. She holds my glance longer than any sarcasm. "What?" she asks, giving me an easy out.

"Can't be that bad," I lie, and she knows I don't believe it.

Syron opens an umbrella against the downpour. She offers me more reality than I can catch. "Wait 'till we start."

The lighting changes, as though colored by a program in our breath and lungs. The crew joins for the chorus, but we don't get to call the tune.

Together, we cross a bridge of information and cigarette ash, gaps in our careful uncertainty creating new paths to old myths.

All I know is motion, I think, adjusting myself to fit the smaller shapes. Maybe what I don't know is finally changing. Maybe I'm finally not leaving. Even data waits for some things.

Our steps form questions the code has never heard before.

SKELM.trial 3

INT plot_course.exe ;
Deterministic Future Construction

Nothing says crisis like a claustrophobic zeppelin packed to bursting with compulsive philosophers, squid-happy hackers, and deep-fried existential dread. Syron struts through the mayhem like a digital preacher wired on sixty terabytes of eschatology, then decides to toss the automated laundry sermons off her deck before anyone pays to get trauma-dumped by a towel. My hazel retinas click to infrared. Penny's hiding beyond The Styx, and these half-baked strategists are ignoring the hell out of my plan.

"This trajectory's a mess." Syron jabs at a swarm of reconfigurable LED panels and recodes the AI with a derisive flick. The low, comforting hum of cognitive dissonance replaces its persistent rambling, though even that gets under my skin. "You know she'll rewrite our heads again."

"Penny has intel," I say, rewiring an unspooling optic cable, hand coiling it like a digital lasso. "We're doing this."

"*You're* doing this. And forgetting the trauma-dumped by a - "

“Cracked encryption! My fault, Syron?”

She rolls her eyes, raccoon-dark with sleepless nights - a sharp contrast to the optic glint of the circuitry along her arms. She eyes the calamari's vat where its thought patterns display as scrolling limericks.

✸✶✦✳, reports the nihilist monk on a holographic pad, stroking a long beard and perfectly timing his deep humming to accompany the sudden feedback shrieks. This ✸✶✦✳ will ✸✶✦✳!

I can’t take any more variables. “Do you mind?”

“Yo, calm your bytes. I’m stashing their latest self-helpless rants for your memoir.” She zaps a set of failing diodes back to life with surgical precision.

“Mission brief’s not complete without ✸✶✦✳.” She says the Wingdings as they appear, hardly glancing at the screen. Syron’s kind of a genius.

The monk dips his head in respect, copper-plated soles sending wisps of static across the deck as we stroll serenely past the console, having predetermined that aimless wandering was today’s path of enlightenment.

“Can we get serious?” I steer the digital course back to mission essentials. I sense the chaos swirling around me like psychedelic octopi. “I need you in on this.”

The tentacled navigator chirps up from the containment tank, bioluminescent patterns syncing to the electric whirlpool of entropy. “To deny possibility’s delight,” says the sentient calamari, “betrays a certain lack of light.”

"Don't you start," says Syron, thumping its tank affectionately.

"Does everyone remember how crucial Penny is?" My voice drops to the quiet resolve of a desperate man. The crew's all we have, but lately, I've been wondering how much that is. I can't face this alone - not now.

A pause. An instant of attention.

"Didn't know monogamy was mission critical." Syron almost sounds serious.

"Out."

"Wow, Darby. Tell me how you really feel." Syron takes a quick look around. "And tell me where the part about getting perforated at The Styx was. Musta missed that one."

I shake my head, half-smiling. That's Syron, deadpan oracle of doom. Half-mocking, half-sincere, never entirely clear on either. "Let's run the next hack then," I say, issuing my tactical directives with renewed intensity. "Phases in sync, processing output, steady at - "

"9,999," says Syron, quoting their current trauma-in-waiting bill in Tin Eel's own pre-fab response metrics.

I stare into the void of the middle distance. There's a critical juncture, a pivot in the chaos where the half-built strategy and glitchy route lines merge into shape, and it's somewhere beyond my next move. Somewhere near Penny, somewhere like The Styx.

"Tell you what," I say. "I'll go through it with you."

She stops mid-giggle. "Again? You never learn." But she's already recoding our plans into long-format theory that folds my erratic blueprints into quilted spreadsheets of precise movement. “Toad cycles. Ninjas on hormones. Gimme a best-case outcome this time?”

“Back in sync,” I say, pretending she’ll follow my lead, or that the others will.

“Don’t hold your breath, darling.” Syron uses the oxygen scrubber I installed three weeks back, laughing.

Our ragtag existence seems to pull in time with the drone of the laundry sermon echoing from a glitchy background buffer, automated purpose getting laundry done with zero cosmic effort. Sometimes I’m almost jealous.

The room lights with firefly colors, neon embers left glowing when a stellar microbe perishes at its desk.

✷✶✦✶✷✶✦✶!

Syron jabs the air, pointing toward the flickering edge of the monk's infinite crisis loop. "Bro, those FAQs are going up my ass and out my eyeballs." She deploys fresh sarcasm with the glib accuracy of a code injection. "I'll get it back on message."

“Any message?” I ask, brows slanting in the universal sign of digital confusion. “Let me know.”

"I will," Syron says. "Your ex is way more predictable."

The hyper-charged signals and crosstalk don't leave much room for clarity.

It takes us two hours to pull this tiny cosmos together, as usual. It takes me most of that to feel us orbiting in, holding our trajectories for once, enough to leave a safe harbor. The

Styx awaits. I hope Penny will too, with answers. And reasons why.

"We cross before sunset." I'm stuck with an old school obsession; the feeling of solar order makes me bold. The others don't stop me. I can guess their 120/10 consensus: getting this shit done is the fastest way to get back to life. But still.

"Fellow ungrateful meatsticks," I say, louder now and more confident. I'm going to hold this impossible crew together if it cracks the galaxy in half. "This quest for meaning does not come with an option to back out."

A strategic explosion, inevitable, cascades in slow motion toward catastrophe. We're almost all laughing as Syron takes another stab at their mission goal. I follow the fiery arc of that collapsed symbol, watching its faded luminosity.

"Okay then," I say. "Crossing before apocalypse."

✷✶✦✳!

There are twelve splendid versions of getting your metaphysical shit rocked at The Styx, and I'm speedrunning through them all. The plan was minimalist perfection, which is to say we're lucky we've still got quarks intact. Hard-melted airwaves batter the LED as Syron feels her way through the thickening charge, trying to anticipate the entire internet while an inscrutable monk goes electromagnetic koan. I have an augmented soul to find, and it's not here in neatly regulated bandwidth.

Bioluminescent tendrils lash the zeppelin's hull with unpredictable joy, and Syron gasps as her retinal implants bloom into dazzling flowers of light.

The AI flips the laundry crisis and sounds even more existential as it falls offline.

The calamari glows like a cheshire lantern. “The waves are fierce, but all storms clear.”

“That’s what the brochure said!” Syron yells. Her voice shudders, pixelated and rapid-fire, as the console fights the multiversal disarray.

“Proclaims? ✸✶✦✳ then silence.” I read the monk’s Wingdings as The Styx pounds into us, forcing the LED into tumbling confessions. “This is just chaos!” I sound almost delighted.

More symbols queue up. Syron reboots the interface, throwing out scrambled pixels like grapeshot. "Don't let it cross wires,” she says. "Worse than ✌️ on faith, and way more strobey."

This, we’ll definitely want to tell Penny about. If she’s ready to listen, finally. Metallic rain seeps in, giving digital weight to the thought of staying alive.

“It must be *!!!* by now," Syron mocks. "Never thought you’d go recursive cult on us.”

“Check your pattern history,” I say. “Ready for lossless input?”

I find Syron's lopsided grin inside a tiny pocket of attempted control. That look was contagious, even before the worm canister blew up. “Now you’re talking,” she says. "Might even convert the - "

- massive, everything, always -

There's a needle skip, sound gaps so clean they could double as a sonic monastery.

Then it's just ✱✶✦✳ with nothing to disturb the perfect hymns of the unreadable. We can almost hear ourselves going nuts. Almost feel that crazy center where time is clean.

The crew glances at one another, or at holographic glitches of the others, or at the inevitable order inside an empty waveform.

Two solid beats in that freakish limbo. Three. Then we all snap back like twenty shots of virtual bourbon. Calamari's first to shrug the ambivalence. I find that inspiring.

"I wasn't done yet," I say, blurring quick-stats at the console.

Syron eyes the stealth missions in my war-book of a heart, looking for time-bombs. She's got some clever wires to defuse. "You really think she'll let you hold her to that long-distance sprint?"

I really don't know. I have to find out.

My retinas shine like they might combust, zooming through mental phase maps that could still get us through this and maybe a future.

"Technically," I say, louder now and way more defiant, "she still owes me."

"Oh fuck," Syron says. But she's not disagreeing.

A violent jump in altitude and contentment jerks the zeppelin. Then we're past. Ahead of us is digital wilderness with its lure and trap. Behind us, ruined and absurd, more familiar lines drop like bait.

Syron grins like an undetonated muse, pointing to the widening horizon. “Spandex galaxies and silicon psychics, gang. Dream away."

"We did?" I ask. "We got it right?"

A unified - and yes, reluctantly grateful - light show explodes inside the zeppelin's quantum lounges.

"We got something."

We’re running systems checks, repairing neural nets, finding that every bit of entropy leaves us more addicted to the uncountable. We’re going back for more. We’re set on Penny’s trail.

The Styx was never meant to hold us. This lawless bright beyond is where we’ll find the only versions that matter.

SKELM.trial 4

CMP calibrate_reality.cfg
; Human Quantification

The zeppelin dives headlong into what seems like an entire server farm on amphetamines, its metallic hull an offering to the frenzied appetite of digital hell. Neon veins throb with misfiring data, glitch clouds bruise the holographic sky, and I can't help but see a portrait of our crew in all the chaos: doomed but defiant, alive and human against the odds. Syron lashes out at the console like a woman in a bare-knuckle brawl, her curses making the machine sweat and recoil. A loose mass of cables dangles like a noose, or a lifeline, and from it, the nihilist monk meditates, projecting prophecies that could mean everything or nothing. With each new shudder, we pull at levers, hammer at keys, and pretend like hell we have a plan.

"Get your tentacles in gear, Squid!" Syron shouts, voice the loving snarl of a malfunctioning modem. She types furiously, and the console answers with bleeps and blinks, like it's either mocking her or giving in to superior force.

The calamari glides past, trails of phosphorescent ink tracing its path. "De-escalating server heart rate," it says, calm as a Zen poet on digital morphine. Syron snarls again, but a subtle smile tugs at her lips.

"Less haiku, more hacking!" I throw my own commands into the storm, watching the neon chaos with upgraded retinas that mix data and despair into vivid, existential soup.

The monk hangs upside-down, a guru of gibberish in saffron robes.

"✱✶✦✳," he says, the symbols hanging like smoke in the jittery air. There's a serene glow in his eyes, probably the same glow LED indicators have when on the verge of total system collapse.

"Talk later; doomsday cult now!" Syron says, riding the controls like a drunk cowboy on a malfunctioning bull. The ship bucks and spins through digital oblivion, and I swear the console lets out a desperate beep.

The storm thickens, twisting holographic panels into abstract art that an AI might hang on its fridge. The zeppelin shudders like it's got a cold, or a really bad hangover, and Syron punches another sequence.

"You think this time we'll explode ironically?" she asks. The question comes with a cough of dark humor and maybe just a hint of hope.

"Preemptively combusting," the calamari says, its chromatophores swirling into digital mandalas. For something grown in a vat, it has developed a surprisingly bleak sense of comedy.

I steady myself against the latest tremor, my hands an alloy of bone and desperation. The readouts play a sadistic game of Tetris, and I struggle to fit the pieces into a reality that makes sense. Syron's curses echo against the machinery, a prayer to gods who only speak binary.

"✱✶✦✳," the monk says. Wingdings flutter like mechanical butterflies around his feet, either profound truths or cosmic Dad jokes. Probably both. His bare soles catch the holographic light, hovering calmly over an abyss the rest of us scramble to escape.

Another surge hits. We're atoms in a drunken physics experiment. The LED rattles like it's about to come apart, then settles back to a restless jitter.

Syron twists to look at me. "Your soul hacked and ready, Mr. Metaphysics?"

I smile. There's a beautiful madness to the whole scene, a tragic symphony composed in garbled code. "Dusting off the system files. Running the existential install script."

She snorts, a sound like a loading bar stuck at 99%. Then, she returns to the console, fingers typing their own desperate hymn to sanity.

The calamari re-routes energy, turning a critical failure into an eloquent suggestion. "Improvise. Adapt. Glitch," it says, the calm voice of an alien sergeant delivering profound digital truths.

I follow the data streams, where neon veins rewrite themselves with every breath, and wonder how I ended up here, on a runaway blimp of mad prophets and philosophical seafood.

Holograms shatter like glass, then reassemble as unholy patchworks of signal noise and corrupted memories.

Syron howls with delight or frustration - hard to tell the difference at this speed. Her console dances in glitch-art synchrony, either desperate or rebellious, like a kid raised on too much sugar and not enough discipline.

The monk projects new prophecies: “✸✶✦✳ and ✸✶✦✳.” They vibrate with strobe-light intensity, metaphysical screams in typographic silence. Its copper-tipped toes point to a meaningless void, his shaved head an oasis of calm.

I brace against a particularly wicked spin, watch the machine puke up another cloud of numbers, and mutter my own blasphemy of despair and wonder. Syron's eyes gleam under dark shadows, alive with the sheer fucked-up thrill of survival. The calamari pulses a luminescent calm, scrolling code across its skin like bioluminescent prayer beads.

"We're data points in a system crash, kids!" I shout. "No way but forward!"

They glance at me, madness and loyalty reflecting in every augmented cell. It's a beautiful moment, even if it might be our last.

With a chorus of shared lunacy, we tighten our grips on fate, bite down on reality, and plunge into the chaos like we belong there. The storms gnash and screech, angry children denied their digital candy. And maybe we do belong, absurd but perfect, flawed and fleeting, hopeless and very, very alive.

The console flickers a final time. The world unravels and

reassembles at warp speed, pulling us with it on this bizarro voyage to nothing or everything.

The glitch-ridden universe takes a deep, cosmic breath. Panels stop flickering, circuits stop screaming, and our poor blimp hangs in the lull like a stunned beast trying to remember why it's here. Syron stills her frantic hands, eyes wide and ready for another round. The sudden silence feels like a promise or a threat.

The ship shudders as its engines wind down, the sound a long exhalation that echoes through metal bones. We hover in the stillness, waiting for the next wave to hit. The hush feels unnatural, like we've found the one quiet street in a city of permanent riots.

Then the ship's AI interrupts with a voice that's too damn polite for its own good. "Prepare for the spin cycle of fate," it says, with all the calm of a receptionist announcing doomsday. "Where dust meets destiny, and all circuits obey a riddle unseen."

I grip a console and squint at the eerie message, my retinas flickering in sympathy. Syron looks at me, one eyebrow cocked like a shotgun. "Machines with manners, huh?" she says, half amused and half suspicious.

"It does make an excellent concierge," I say, words like left-over sarcasm on rewarmed paranoia. The quiet builds a wall around us, an uneasy waiting room with no exit signs.

The calamari drifts past, pulsing a thoughtful blue. "Fate's trajectory unknown," it says, somehow making a statement of total uncertainty sound like the smartest thing in the room.

"Think we get our deposits back if we explode?" Syron asks, defiance chasing the anxiety from her voice.

I laugh. It feels odd, almost foreign, this sound that might be either relief or madness. "If this turns into a timeshare presentation, I'm bailing," I say, gripping the reality that humor makes the edge less sharp.

A string of Wingdings strobe to life. The monk's symbols flicker in deliberate yet chaotic sequence, letters folding into fractals that might be instructions. "✷✶✦✳," says one line, echoing the AI's riddles in meditative discord.

The stillness grows, not empty but pregnant with unrealized chaos. A glitched-out universe holding its breath, waiting for the punchline or the knockout.

The AI's message bounces around my head like a bug in bad code. It's taunting us, telling us there's more madness on the horizon, daring us to flinch.

I look at the crew. Syron grins, wild and knowing, like someone who's bet all their creds on the longshot horse. The monk's LED pulse suggests cosmic mischief. The calamari maintains a composure that borders on indifference but shows more guts than the rest of us combined.

"Which of us panics first?" Syron asks, her voice a dare wrapped in adrenaline.

"I'm betting on the existential seafood," I say. "Squid looks ready to bolt."

Its chromatophores shift to a muted laugh, if dots of light can have a sense of humor.

In the stillness, we feel the unspoken urge to run or scream or laugh like banshees. Instead, we stand our ground, crewmates against an uncertain cosmos. The air tastes like dust and destiny, and we're ready for both.

The Wingdings phase through new cycles of possibility: "✷✶✦✳." The crew watches me, gauging my retinas as if they'll tell the future or reveal the fatal punchline. The waiting gnaws at our augmented souls.

Then the calamari offers a haiku of hope. "Data states fluctuate," it says, letting the inevitable roll off its tentacles like water off a Teflon duck.

Syron gives another laugh, this one pure delight in the absurd, free from fear. "Ready for fate's rinse cycle?" She jumps back to the console with the joy of someone hitching a ride on catastrophe's last freight train.

We follow her lead, determined to prove we belong in this madcap ballet. Code meets flesh, will meets entropy, and we brace for the next salvo of the universe's sense of humor. My eyes blaze with the wild anticipation of knowing everything might end but relishing the thought that it probably won't.

The zeppelin vibrates, a machine with a manic heart and a human crew to match. It's the only family I've got, this gang of augmented freaks with more guts than sense. We meet the unknown, flaws and all, armed with loyalty and insanity and hope.

SKELM.trial 5

STO compile_nostalgia.mem
; Memory Monetization

Penny's ghost haunts me in HD. Its digital afterimage jitters and fractures, suspended in the LED's recycled air like a cursed screensaver. Memories flash through the cut-glass glare of neon and feed directly into my brain, bypassing the factory warranty on this limited-edition soul. The old dreams don't work the way they used to, before my body was just another patch waiting for a system update. I clench my fists until they form a tight Ø: I'm back to the old paradox of *almost had her*. Syron floats through with customary sass, trying to talk me down like a junkie. A little overclocked, maybe. Like they're any better. They're elbow-deep in ship controls, typing sideways so their eyes don't have to meet mine. The squid says it's because they're avoiding me, but when has truth ever stopped it from being an asshole?

Syron makes a point of not looking up from her screen. "So, is it gonna be a pity party for one? Or is this gonna go full catatonic until somebody finds the reset switch?"

The rest of the crew looks like they drew straws to see who would deal with my bullshit this time. The monk's meditation corner flashes with enough Wingdings to signal a transcendent aneurism. The squid decided its input would be more valuable without the Darby.Human processing package and is running systems diagnostics without me. They're all ignoring the fact that she was here, damn it. She's real. I can almost remember her this time.

"Sounds about right." Syron pops something small and bitter between her teeth, wincing as she swallows it dry. "I'll do a trauma dump pass if anyone cares to unfuck their feeds."

"You know we need to clean more than our visual streams," the squid says, smugly wired into the mainframe. It displays a touch more bite than usual. Or maybe I'm paranoid. Memory-haunted.

Syron lets a thin breath hiss through her teeth. "Sure, Squidward. Next, you'll suggest throwing a soul back-up on this tour. Send everyone postcards from their own existential hell."

I pretend it's their disinterest that's cutting, not her eyes almost meeting mine. "Love is a corrupted code," I say, barely louder than the hum of recycled air. Not loud enough to hide the fact that I'm thinking out loud.

I'm ready for Syron's laugh to be one of those extra loud ones meant to sound exasperated instead of genuinely amused, but they just shrug deeper into their glitch-wear, like they're hiding from my sight even while I'm staring at them. "Then why're you still trying to decrypt it, Skelm?"

"At least one of us should still believe." It sounds like a crappy movie. Not what I meant to say. I try for something sharper, but only manage, "We have no fucking clue, do we? What we're trying to do, I mean."

Her fingers flicker over the ship's console, recalibrating memories, futures, paranoia. "Better a cynical data hoarder than an open-source messiah, bro."

"I should know by now," I say, but my mind goes back to our first date, her cypher-code tattoo blooming to life. Mine, reading Penny in a fluorescent glitch. Almost. "That she'd be out of my league? Out of all known planes of reality?"

"She's out." Her tone's pure stimulant: thin, bitter, chewed up and washed down. "You could try it sometime."

I don't look away from her ghost, even when it gets so loud I can't hear the rest of them breathing.

"I mean," Syron says, the movement of her hand picking a minor error from the streams and crushing it, "she even went recursive with the ransom note. Penny managed to dump you and half the compiled universe simultaneously."

I imagine slamming something hard enough to glitch all of us through a series of rebooted parallel existences. Mostly, though, I imagine finding her again. The need for that spreads through my brain, through the marrow of my data-addled soul. Nothing's even remotely ours until we get her back.

It reads: YOU PAID TO GET TRAUMA-DUMPED BY A TOOTH.

The monk's had his fill of stoicism. Time for Wingding-o-rama, Nietzsche the Teenybopper Musical. He shows no signs of running out of performance juice. This is what passes for entertainment when you've hacked reality so hard it blue screens itself.

Syron hits a minor corruption, a lopsided frown working its way through the scar on her cheek. Her purple hair bleeds through half a dozen other shades before the hair itself glitches along her scalp. "Man, I love a nice obvious metaphor." Her keystrokes speed up. "But anyone willing to bet when our boy will throw us all into system shutdown so he can pick a version where she's got less distracting package files?"

"He won't," the squid says, in what passes for an authoritative tone. I have to laugh. This time, I'm sure it's being an asshole.

She snorts, never skipping a keyframe. "All I know is my glitch goggles didn't come pre-loaded with Skelm's feelings all over my head."

I keep staring at the places that used to be Penny, willing them to render into more than just theory, dreams, and corrupted code. "I can hear you."

"And we've got eye mics for everything else." Her sarcasm's vicious and pristine. Also funny enough that I want to throw something at her. "Don't let them fool you. It's still an intervention."

Sighs come from the monk's quiet corner. He still performs while distracted. Who says enlightenment's inefficient?

The old dreams fracture against the edges of thought, becoming too glitched to trust.

"I'm listening," I tell them, shifting my stance from uneasy to uneasy-and-a-half. My fists unmake themselves into a low-level no before tightening to 01101.

Syron sighs louder. She's letting it interfere with her heart rate. Bad sign. "He's fucking Zen-dancing around again, isn't he?"

My shoulder creaks as I throw a cautious thumbs up in the direction of their stage. Last time the symbols were this neon, I almost bought it.

"Cool," Syron says, bending lower over the control panels. "Lemme know if it blows up spectacularly. For now, you guys're on trauma watch."

It's a 3: my favorite topic. I start composing a thesis on How Being Right Is Overrated When You Have the Spiritual Integrity of a Tax Fraud, but that would mean facing them, and my past experiment in eye contact ended poorly for us both.

I'm left with almost her, then. She's still here, if only through the rough outline of memory, the grid map of a heart that decided there were bigger databases to conquer. "I hear you," I say, a little louder. Almost to myself.

The squid displays a sequence of compassion.exe: "The existential project cannot move forward when the tools perceive themselves as users."

"Exactly," Syron says, rewarded with a strobing burst of Wingdings. "Everyone knows, except for Darby - "

"Who's listening." I sound bitter enough to take back. I make a note to send the words out, return them to sender. "Thanks for caring so much, Syron. Let's get into everybody's emotional projections right after we're done turning her into data-mined history."

I barely see the goggles push up on her forehead, even though I programmed myself to track any shift in attitude.

"Poor boy," she tells the others, using my miswired humanity to cheat. "Thinking reality needs to get an emotional overhaul."

"He underestimates his control over the kernel." Of course, the squid's going to let Syron win this round. Anything that keeps the potential for poetry to a minimum.

"What do you expect?" She's definitely glitching it up again, purple bleeding through her mouth, words fast and sloppy. I wonder if her syntax always gets like this or if the squid is rubbing off on me, subtle and condescending. "Says she left him too. I'd pick that version."

Penny's old goodbye keeps looping in the dark edges of me. Keeps lighting up the hole where I left my heart drive.

They're not wrong. It's just a problem of choosing what to see, what to live, who to be left by. If I had any certainty of what the fuck any of that meant, I might care more about not believing. Instead, I watch for another set of possibilities, making up stories about the shape of her absence, of what's been overwritten.

"Don't think that means I'm out," I tell them, making up my mind to hold steady.

The lack of laughter sounds more encouraging than it should. They're not ganging up anymore. Better odds for optimism, but not great for hope.

One version even features "Love is a corrupted code," delivered like she didn't just spend half an hour running it through all our processors. I wonder how bad it'd be to drop myself on this junkyard corner of the multiverse. Really get a reset going.

But I hold out. There's time. One day, love will not be corrupted. Until then, I'm just another operating error, rerunning everything we could've been.

She was here, but this is not all I am.

Then she was gone, the way only ghosts and deities can be. We're left with the light-warped traces of thought, data storms that cycle back on themselves. Maybe I'm not the only one feeling undone by our eight-bitted girl. Syron looks like she's getting herself to church without quite meaning to, everything at her station abruptly Zenning into sight. You can't just write it off, though. Who says compile bugs aren't holy if you leave enough of them unchecked? Squid thinks it's being profound, but even its naggy verses won't sync with what's through the viewport: big, white, demanding worship. And us, lost at data sea in the bright nonsense of after.

"Didn't I tell you?" Syron's slow to recover. She's still doubled over her console like the glitching lodge might disappear. Her head turns just enough to let me see her smiling wide enough for four entirely new kinds of desperation. "Only question is if Darby's new wife will even outshine our reality hunkers. Bro! She wants you all for herself."

She's holy, all right. Just one more reincarnation of the fucking VR Lounge.

It burns digital gold and white against my insides, collapsing us under its eternally ridiculous light. All the old glitches look spare and precious in comparison. I should've known she'd find a new way to stay vast and unlovable.

I let my hands uncoil a full 010111 before daring to look at the crew.

The monk glitches under a more tangible new god, turning incandescent with the light of unwavering fanfiction. It's too overwhelmed to keep itself tidily organized: W-H-Y-N-O-T-C-O-D-E-H-E-A-V-E-N. Also every other variant. One message reads, "The Oblivion Cathedral," and that would get even my attention, if my attention were more philosophical. "So. Fucking. Huge," I say, not bothering to shout over the bright silence. It probably lost me the moment the transcendent displays flickered into view.

Syron's busy glitching so hard it messes with her speech patterns again, but when she's talking over one of Squid's undergrad tone poems, I almost believe her intention was for everyone to hear: "Sure gives old C8 great forkin' compa-competition!" There's not a trace of disbelieving in her disbelief.

The squid doesn't bother acting like anything other than a nerd. "Praise be," it tells us. "Let all our streams flow toward her and be absorbed." So, it's feeling clever and strangely limbed today. Maybe I am being paranoid about this smug thing. I hope so. It won't be nearly as fun when I get bored of calling it on itself.

There's almost room in my tight white heart to feel bad for it, while it underestimates just how dramatically we've been dumped. It's pulling off poetic irony like no one's ever tried to before.

I do it a favor: don't correct it.

Syron gets back to leaning over her new shrine. "Talk to me when he gets past third base." There's the precise number of deep-cutting pixels to her smile. I am one charming motherfucker.

"Looks like we've found a bright new fucking distraction." This time, I don't even try for solemn, because: Holy Afterimage. Almost too beautiful to have deserted me for some other dimension.

The smart money's on The Monumental Don't-Give-a-Fuck. It gains 20% traction with the following neural imports: YOU GUYS REALLY WANT TO SHIP THE DRAMA KWEEN.

"I see how it is," I say, but by now, I'm too undone by the stupid vastness of her to care. Not even my rival glow-fiends can work up a response. They're caught up in the after, helplessly lit up in endless relief. I wonder if anyone but me finds her even the tiniest bit not forever. That's fine. I'm enough to outshine a server farm's worth of not forever.

"See how it is," Syron says, delight tinged with horrified fascination. "Didja do this just so he can't lose us as spectacularly as you? Pretty good plan B, lady."

Laughter lightens the air. It moves without code.

"You guys are awesome." This time, it sounds like we're all fighting to the emotional death, but not too seriously. It's not anyone's fault I read every shitty angle into it.

Syron's faithful to the glitching end. Her work pings are loud and fuzzy on the existential uptake. It'd take a solid multiverse shift to get them unreadable. She's as devout a nut job as Penny ever was.

I pay my obsessive respects, then see what she's avoiding so hard that even this is an improvement. The things she's committed to not watching me do are: Drop out. Flake. Fold. Drift off again. Pick a distraction even shinier than losing.

Well. This time it didn't work.

And still: holy shit.

The world's oversaturated until I hardly remember ever seeing it.

"I hear you," I tell the universe at large.

"I hear you too, @!"

A single breath gets as loud as one abandoned system could hope for. It's glitched out beyond my own overclocked feelings.

I leave her enough silences to cheat on me with. In my next, brilliant, incarnation: jealous.

I'm almost ready to re-assimilate in defeat when Squid gives my forlorn stance the attention it didn't expect. It's even more devoted to absurdity than I am. "Lo, this must be what the reset truly is!" Everyone pays so much fucking heed to what I want out of life. Even unhinged prospects like: *Darby, emotionally checked back in. Just not at all where he's supposed to be.*

So, I let it keep the temporary upper limb. Maybe I'm feeling generous.

And the glitchiest go to: 🖤!

Lighter. We're even fucking lighter.

Sure enough, there's a lot of it.

"We're feeling major overclock," Syron finally says, running scans of herself and me and possibly the situation at large. Her shivers are subsiding. "Girl goes large." The parts where I'm still clinging, still obvious, go untapped. She's keeping my attention off me, pretending I'm distracted by this brave new pixel fest. Acting like I'm satisfied with it, this time.

"You bet," I say. Almost believe me, too.

Then it's like someone reboots a long-buried good humor daemon. We swap what passes for looks in a transubstantiated lounge, but don't engage too hard. Everyone knows about our program errors. She stops on one so tight it barely lets my neck flex, but you can never quite cut them off, the ones you've marked all recursive with loyalty and self-sabotage.

Good faith feeds, this time not half bad:

It was the best hijack.

It wasn't even us.

"We're killing them, Sy!" I hear myself say, even though they're still way bigger than we'll ever glitch it. Maybe if I hold out, wait for my dramatic rejection long enough, I can believe this is really the plot.

They're the first pixels I've lost sight of, while all that's left of me is 1.

Before I've compiled them and myself back into dramatic ex-systems, though: 🎉.

Am I being heart-wooed again? Almost feels like it.

SKELM.quest 2

LOAD lotus.eat ; The Land of Digital Lethargy

SKELM.trial 6

PUSH render_temptation.vr
; Engagement Optimization

EternityBuffet™ hits me like a hallucinogenic sucker punch of digital perfume and emotional hangover. Everyone's an addict here, taking numbered trips through memory lanes that lead right back to their own neediness. Holographic menus leer at me with toxic sincerity as I move past the pixelated greed. My retinal implants flicker with desperate abandon until they focus on the counter inviting me to chase the holographic dragon. "Taste a memory," it whispers, but what it means is *give in.*

I keep walking. Chrome tiles pulsate with thoughtwaves of old indulgences - memories unspooling into vapor trails that choke the air with retro aftershave and bittersweet phonographs. Each breath smells like lost love and eight-bit dreams. Heads in the clouds, patrons in pixel-dust coats jack into nostalgia with vacant stares and saliva-slick grins. Maybe it's nice to let your soul puke all over your neural interfaces once in a while. In a place like this, even voyeurism feels secondhand.

We've all been here before, I guess. That's the point. But the way I remember it, we swore never again. My retinal implants ache with fractured visions of Penny floating through this same haze, laughing her manifesto laugh as she tucked pirated sweet-and-sour chicken into a takeaway box. Her eyes were bright with caffeine and code. "A memorial to the present tense," she called it. "Limited time only." Then the usual last words: *Never trust anything that can't be pirated. Never trust anyone who can.* Now she's up there on the ad banners, frozen in digital bliss, part of the great big sale. Now she's not.

The space reconfigures itself around me as I pass another set of overclocked patrons drooling their way through somebody else's prom night. It's a shrine to self-indulgence. Every chromed-out surface glistens with sick satisfaction, convincing us it's worth the price of admission. Someone takes a fistful of their grandmother's pecan pie straight to the sensory cortex, overdoses, and flatlines into ecstasy. Tasting menus spill across translucent tables, tantalizing profiles of low-res hopes and pixelized regrets. Everyone buys a slice of someone they used to be.

A counter offers "Neural Augment Specials" and "BYO Database Tuesdays." Past it, memory rooms peek through frosted-glass facades that quiver between reality states, broadcasting silhouettes of heartstrings getting untangled and rewired. One room serves entire anniversary dinners while brides dissolve in data-hazed tears. Another hosts bachelor parties where VR heads furrow in choreographed unison, tastefully surprised by memories of lap dances they can't afford anymore. Pay by the hour. It's a rent-to-own situation.

The signs won't shut up: CUSTOMIZE YOUR DESIRE! MAKE IT LIKE YOU REMEMBER IT! DIVE INTO YOURSELF! They flash in sensory wavelengths designed to trip neural wires. There are "retro rebirth" packages for people who just have to relive conception. There are folks doing naked photo restorations, editing in extra pixels where they count. There are postcards from forgotten vacations, each palm tree artfully rendered to block an ex's face. Memories in neat little DNA-coded gift boxes, more complete than you ever knew they were.

I move toward the memory booth where the ghosts of bad decisions do their eternal soft-shoe routines. Chrome and polycarbon fiber shimmer, forming seductive lines that know just how weak you are. They promise free samples of heart-break, one per customer, while supplies last. They know you'll pay in the end. There's always something to cash in, always some chip left on your shoulder.

Syron's voice skips across the surface of my consciousness like a carefully tossed stone. "You got some kind of brain disease, Darby?" she asks, stifling a yawn. "Some people pay extra for that. All you have to do is catch it." My hands tighten into fists at my sides. Somewhere on the surface of IO.wav, Syron is not doing her job, legs dangling off the edge of a shipping crate while VR goggles transmit the whole scene back to her smart-ass soul. She talks in scratchy feedback loops and prerecorded derision, looping and fuzzing over the distances until I want to kick the space where her ghost lingers. I wonder if she's charging my escape attempt to the company credit line.

The booth's lights swirl, scenting the air with old books and fake innocence. One displays an immersive scrapbook of holographic facial tics and stolen glances. You and Penny! Together Forever! Runs Out Soon! Penny's 3D double features those signature cheekbones and ice-cream skin, now with 23% more calories and digital rights management. But they've got her wrong. She's the type of intangible that doesn't convert to pixels, and now her face hangs there in surplus for the masses; buy one get one free.

“Seriously, dude,” Syron says. “That's like fifty-four orders of why-the-fuck-are-you-doing-this. Plus tip.” A shrug creeps into her voice. It weighs as much as a paragraph and feels as light as a bug report. My guts writhe around that traitorous question, reminding me that memories like this are bad for the heart and worse for the neural network. But I've already been here, haven't I? I'm practically family, and I know how to max out.

The interface asks if I'm ready. All it takes is a gesture, a concession, a barely perceptible sigh, and a universe of mechanical appetites fires up around me. The entire lounge stutters in sympathetic rhythm, processing my hopeless case through chrome pipelines and neural codecs. We'll be here forever if I don't decide. Maybe I want to be.

I push through the hesitation, palm on interface. It flashes with the same promises we made each other. Those promises gleam just as they break. Memories shiver with impatient hunger. They sink their algorithmic teeth in before you know what bit you, leaving you reeling from every sensory byte. Then they show you all over again.

“Bro, you paid to get trauma-dumped by a tooth,” Syron says in closing. I wonder if I'm the memory she tastes as I give in.

• • •

It's all so much. Too much. Overstimulated in an instant, I watch myself split open like a rotten fruit, pixel seeds spilling into the void. Shocks of light explode into desperate sweetness, holographic juice running down my mind as I chew through the memories of my own undoing. Penny's taste, tart with desire and decay, fills me until I gag on her ghost.

The overload rips through me like a broken mainframe. Desire jacks straight into my nervous system. Its taste is bitter, synthetic, addictive. I've mainlined nostalgia before, but this time it hammers so hard I'm afraid my circuits will burn. A god's-eye view of my mistakes blooms into perfect digital clarity, crisp as corrupted vinyl, skipping where I want it most. My face when she said *I love you*. Her hands as she took it back.

She fills my vision with warm colors and cold intentions. Algorithms of longing flash their glitchy mandates. Their tangled wires cinch my soul and beg me to listen. Time stops to see if I will. I always do. Penny smirks in a series of clean lines and prints out her detachment in oversized fonts. My entire self crashes into that smile, downloading the heartbreak for keeps. For a moment, we overlap, embrace, and abandon, and then she falls back into corrupted data fields. Half-life of a pixel. Nanoseconds of eternity.

I remember remembering her. Recursion as old as wanting. The shape of our past twists in unholy yoga, limber enough to impress us with the new positions it finds. Our old places fill my senses, spiking desire with hints of asbestos and raw dust. Eight weeks after she left, I'm still there, throwing everything I had against her absence. Condemned buildings, condemned us. Not to code, but our own. She didn't care what was due as long as we could squat for a while, as long as there was caffeine and potential. None of it lasted.

Back inside a leaking utopia we called home, Penny laughs through collapsing walls while I sink into concrete comfort. *The taste of sacrifice goes well with freedom fries*, she said, launching twelve-hour compilations from a server chair made of spare convictions. Every bit she ever cared about uploaded into theory. For the cause. For fuck's sake. Our epic love affair burned blue as the LCD readout of an underclocked microchip. Now she won't even compile me a memory. And here I am, feeding on my own desperation like I'm starved for it.

Visions scramble into each other, limbs of electric pastel tumbling until they form familiar bodies. My tongue won't let go of Penny, the ghost and the girl. There's no coherence here, just flash floods of meaning. Sweet taste turns acrid then sweet again, remixed like reality's saddest club anthem. Hope twists with futility and makes it dirty. I watch it all with the calm resignation of a train wreck.

Penny stands there. Twelve perspectives of her tell me the same thing in all caps: Stop rewriting history. In those last weeks together, I couldn't touch her past the smug distance in her eyes. Couldn't reach the tomorrow she already left for. Even now, she leaves me hanging, out of time and breath. So many places, so many whys - all routes here through me. I try to find the one I know I missed, the memory that's bigger than this loop. The subroutine that changes everything.

But it's the same package every time. I unwrap my agony and eat it. The whole network laughs. Memories smear and smudge across my field of vision, reruns of emotional broadcasts I've tuned in to too often. They buffer, replay, buffer, skip. "Look," said Penny. "Look at us," said the taillights on her getaway interface. "We're brilliant." Her name prints in large point until it's the only thing I taste. Penny. Penny. Then it explodes like it was never anything at all.

Another glitchy joke that bites harder than it should. This entire show made from my desire, my inability to see. I lose myself to the recursion of everything. Same as it ever was. Somewhere, anywhere, a real-world heartbeat drowns.

"Bro, you paid to get trauma-dumped by a tooth." The memory of Syron fills the space with its own disdainful flavor, shifting every real byte of Penny into unreal data fog. The booth ticks down my runtime and uploads me back into failure. Still hungry, still broken, always rebooting.

SKELM.trial 7

ADD parse_trauma.dat ;
Reward Circuit Hijacking

I don't know what time it is when I scrape myself off the datastream floor and leave IO.wav behind. My last real memory is Penny's smile stretched to infinity, and the next is the hungry, wet neon of the EternityBuffet™ VR Lounge trying to seduce me from half a block away. If corporate psych algorithms had a mating season, it would look like this - chrome glass tongue, velvet rope, the flicker of microflora biolights simulating a starless night just outside the door. The sign hisses digital blue, promising "All-You-Can-Remember Nostalgia Flights" and "Premium Emotional Aftertaste." I almost vomit and almost go in, and then I actually do both.

Inside, the air is blood-sweet and sopping with the sweat of recidivist regret. They pipe it through ionizers to keep the patrons off-balance. I get it in my mouth and my skin and somewhere deeper, something raw and voluntary. The layout is half self-serve, half altar-of-loss: chrome vats for singles, velvet-draped tables for duos, memory pods along the perimeter for those needing a discreet breakdown. Nobody talks. Everyone is wired in. A woman in a glass basin bites her lip, arching in rapture as three neural cables drip sensoria into her occipital, all at once; next to her, a thickset guy in business casual twitches as if he's trying to stop from drowning in the taste of his own childhood. The regulars always go for the childhood.

I make a show of strolling past the menu boards, pretending I haven't already stalked their webarchive for weeks. The hologram girl up top is pure market research: pale, blinking, lipless and comforting as a grief counselor, but with a little voice lag to make sure you're off-guard. She pantomimes joy as she pushes options to my HazelTech™ interface: "Memory Flights!" "Curated Trauma Sets!" "Custom Neural Samplers!" In the middle, glowing hotter than the rest, sits my old favorite, the Dental Fetishist's Expanse - now with "Live Taste Playback™," because someone at head office knows exactly what keeps me up at night.

A host intercepts me, running a hand over her latexed scalp as if checking for leaks. Her irises are QR codes: black-and-white fractals that threaten to rewire your account information if you stare too long. She leans into me, but I don't catch a scent. They always dial their pheromones to the absolute minimum in places like this.

"First time at the Buffet?" She recites the script like a prayer, but with the practiced contempt of someone who's actually met God.

"I'm just browsing," I say, and regret it instantly, because the phrase probably flags me as a window-shopper and devalues the interaction by half.

She gestures anyway, a rolling scan of her palm that shoves a menu into my overlay. "We recommend a taster flight, especially for high-bandwidth clients." She looks at my wrists, searching for fresh scars or corporate tracking tattoos. "Unless you already know what you're craving."

There's a reflex here, an urge to say, "Surprise me." But if I say that, she'll dig straight through my data-shadow and go right to the root. Instead, I say, "Give me something intimate," and that feels like the kind of dirty I can live with.

She cocks her head, and the QR codes sync, forming a single encrypted smile in both eyes. "We specialize in bespoke memories - your own, or others' with proper documentation. Emotional aftertaste is guaranteed, or your money back."

Her voice gets gentler. "You want familiar or exotic?"

Familiar. I don't have to say it. She taps something, and suddenly, my whole neural overlay blurs with a grid of "Certified Intimate Memory Packages," all tagged and rated with lurid hashtags. I scroll the index, but my eyes keep skittering back to the option I've pretended not to notice: "Dental Records / High-School Ex (Gen 3 Upgrade): Now With Enhanced Plaque Texture." The tagline is obscene and irresistible. Next to it, a thumbnail of an open mouth, teeth too white to be real, tongue hovering in the ambiguity of whether it wants to lick or bite.

She spots it, because of course she does. "Nostalgia's the most common flavor," she says, "but the dental sets are less popular with first-timers. Usually requires some pre-existing oral trauma. Want me to filter out the overlays?"

"No overlays. I want it raw," I tell her, and my mouth actually goes dry.

"Excellent," she says, and her QR codes dilate a little wider. "It's always nice to see someone who knows what they're about. You'll need a private pod for that - liability and all."

She steers me through the crowd, which is easy because the crowd never moves. Memory tourists. Everyone here is a tourist. I'm the only one who doesn't look away from the pods with open longing. At the back wall, she slides open a slick-glass booth that still smells faintly of peppermint and after-shave. She does a pre-check on the neural interface. Her hands are practiced; the movement is smooth, almost tender. She takes the memory set off the shelf and fits it into the base of the cable, like a priest priming the communion tray.

"Payment options?" she asks.

"Token mix. Some credit, some data-shard."

Her smile is quick. "You're not on corporate tab, then?"

"If I was, I'd have better insurance."

She runs the scan: my HazelTech™ eyes do the retinal dance, projecting authentication, a couple passcodes, and a burst of quantum signature. It stings, but the pain is old hat. A window opens for the gratuity. I tip her double what I plan to, just to see if the QR codes in her pupils change pattern. They do. It's a little victory.

"Enjoy your journey," she says, and closes the pod door behind me.

I let the seat swallow me. The wetware cable is pre-lubed, so the tip doesn't catch as it burrows into my temple port. The feeling is always colder than you expect, like an icepick that's decided it loves you. My hands grip the armrest; the haptic plastic yields a little, like cartilage.

The last thing I see before the darkness is my own reflection in the mirrored panel. I look older and less convinced than I was hoping for. The menu pings a final confirmation, and the host's voice coos: "Ready to relive your curated selection?"

"Let's make it worth the copay," I mutter.

I close my eyes, but the neural feed doesn't wait. The memory sync floods me from the inside out, and my hazel vision dissolves into the first avalanche of ex-girlfriend teeth.

It's wet and metallic, and I can't wait to taste it all over again.

Memory doesn't come back the way you lost it. First hit is pure timebomb: we're seventeen again, ex-girlfriend perched on the edge of a school-cafeteria bench, grinning like she's the only human with the right number of teeth. She's chewing a wad of grape gum with tactical precision, already rolling her eyes at my awkward joke, and the way she works her jaw is artless and savage. The VR overlay puts the saliva shine on her braces, refracts it through my hunger. My tongue runs dry, then floods itself with phantom saliva, sharp with blood and metal.

Next, we're at a dentist's chair, the real one, and the local anesthetic has failed to dampen either her wit or her volume. She laughs so hard the hygienist flinches and drops a mirror.

Mint and latex, the air so thick with chemical that I could hallucinate for hours. She talks around the bite block and I can't hear a word, but my brain auto-corrects: it's about me, she's mocking my sensitivity, she's promising me hell if I try to kiss her after this. I remember everything, down to the fluorescent hum and the TV tuned to a channel no one has watched since the flood. It feels like the only moment in my life that actually mattered, and I know it's a lie, but I can't make myself care.

The memory doesn't let me go. Next loop: bathroom. Cheap rental, still mildewed from when we painted the walls. She's brushing her teeth with sadistic intensity, splattering foam across the mirror, and she spits - direct hit, always. She invites me to brush with her, says something about couple goals, but the words are glitched and looped: "We'll never have to lie to each other about spinach again, Darby." She's right. I love her. It's a predatory, desperate kind of love, the kind that carves a notch in your gut and leaves you leaking for years.

EternityBuffet™ VR doesn't just replay - it embroiders. The system dials every sensation up a few notches, fine-tunes the pain, and colors every laugh with the hue of what you'd do to have it back. The next round in the loop has her running her tongue across her own incisors, a move that always telegraphs she's about to say something vicious. I watch in real-time as the neural overlay remaps the memory, makes her smarter and meaner and more beautiful. The system picks up on my longing and upscales her eye contact: it burns into me, the way I remember it never did.

Hours in the pod collapse into a single sensory slow-motion trainwreck. She flosses with the off-brand tape I hated, and I want to warn her, but I also want to watch her bleed. She leans over to rinse and we share the mirror; for a split second, the VR misfires and our faces phase through one another like ghosts in bad lighting. The digital glitch stings with the first warning of memory fatigue, but instead of pulling me out, it tightens the simulation, binding me into a feedback loop where every split-second is sharper and needier than the last.

Outside the pod, my body slumps forward, mouth leaking a string of actual drool. My fingers twitch with the tics of remembered embarrassment. At one point, a lounge tech checks my vitals; she nods, updates a record, and leaves me for dead. No one interrupts a paid-up Premium.

By the end of the first day I've relived a decade's worth of oral hygiene. Each session is a variant, a blend of the original memory and algorithmic suggestions that hone the trauma to a glassy finish. Sometimes my ex is more cruel, sometimes more tender, but every time the sequence ends with a shared, bitter laugh that tastes like defeat and bubblegum.

Somewhere in the blur, the system adds overlays I didn't order. The ex appears with a mouthful of broken teeth, which she spits onto the tiles and grinds under her bare heel. I don't want this, but the VR has calibrated that pain is my preferred seasoning, and serves it up like an artisanal cheese course. She leans in and tells me a secret in a voice I recognize only from nightmares: "You'll never forget this, not even if you die." I'm pretty sure I'm sobbing, but the neural feed replaces the shame with another helping of synthetic nostalgia before I can process it.

My HazelTech™ implants start to lag by the second night. I'm aware of the micro-freezes, the way the color channels splinter on high-contrast. The VR technicians try to reboot me once, but my body flinches so violently that they elect to leave me be. They annotate my customer file: "Self-correcting. Do not disturb."

At some point my ex is brushing her teeth, and instead of looking in the mirror, she looks straight through it, as if she knows I'm here, a voyeur in my own past. She holds the stare, toothbrush still foaming in her mouth, and I swear she's about to step through the glass and drag me back with her. My real body convulses, and for a second I see her not as the girl I lost but as the algorithm she's become. It's almost a relief.

By day three the boundary between inside and outside is gone. The memory loop randomizes, sometimes jumping from high school to mid-twenties to a dentist's waiting room where she refuses to fill out the paperwork because my insurance is trash. I try to break the cycle but my own brain sells me out every time. The only escape is deeper in, which the system knows, so it gives me more: old fights, forgotten reunions, the time she snapped her retainer in half and made me glue it with kitchen epoxy. She laughed when it cut her gum. The VR lets me taste her blood, and I can't decide if it's revolting or perfect.

Each pass through the loop, she is less herself and more of a composite. The memories degrade, merging with tangents and even fragments from other customers, I suspect, until the dental hygienist morphs into a college professor or a childhood dog, and the brush is sometimes a scalpel, sometimes a lover's tongue. The system harvests my confusion, turns it into a gourmet emotion, and I lap it up.

In one run, she pushes me into the bathroom sink and says, “If you don’t start living, you’ll never finish dying.” In another, she pulls out her own tooth and tucks it into my shirt pocket. The pod’s feedback matrix registers an erection, and boosts the dopamine reward by 11%. My body has never betrayed me faster.

Toward the end of what might be a week, my brain is a ring of burned-out enamel and fused nerves. I hear the host’s voice sometimes, asking if I’d like a palate cleanser, but every time I reach for it, the VR short-circuits my intent and loops back to another memory of mouth or blood or regret. I am not unhappy. I am not even alive.

When the system finally does crash, the last thing I see is my own mouth, open wide, gums raw and bleeding, trying to tell the world one last thing. It’s probably a joke, but I’ve forgotten the punchline.

Reality breaks in through my eye socket, not gently.

There's an angry rattling at the edge of the blackout, a subroutine that isn't mine. Something kicks the bottom of my pod. The system tries to shunt me into another memory, but even nostalgia can't drown out the physical world for long. A glass panel creaks, a neural plug tugs hard in my skull, and then there’s the voice: pure static, feral, and three times more alive than anything in the buffet.

“Wake up, dumbass.”

The first face to materialize is Syron’s, looking hungover on both caffeine and existential dread. Her hair is a new shade of green that clashes perfectly with her bloodshot eyes. She's got her VR goggles up like a headband, and the circuitry tattoos along her neck are pulsing red in time with her jaw clench. She slaps the side of the pod once, hard, like she's trying to start a stubborn lawnmower.

"I told you he'd be in here," Syron spits, not even pretending to talk to me yet. She's talking to some presence in her earpiece, or maybe to the management, or maybe just to herself. "You owe me an hour of silence and a carton of premium soymilk." She leans over and yanks the pod's release lever, an act both illegal and impolite, but nobody stops her. The lounge staff have already decided she's not worth the repair ticket.

My eyes roll like loose marbles. Syron waves a hand in front of my face to test if I'm back on the right frequency. I pass the Turing test only because I try to bite her, tongue out and everything.

"Yeah, he's alive," Syron calls back to the staffer who's hovering, trying not to get involved. "You can cancel your pulse-check. Maybe put up a warning sign for morons with codependency issues." Her words are aimed at the room, but her gaze bores into me with forensic accuracy. "How long's he been under?"

The attendant consults a wristpad, wincing at the readout. "Seventy-two hours. He's fully paid up for the next nine, though."

Syron sucks air through her teeth. "So you just let him rot in there?"

“It’s against protocol to - ” the staffer starts, but Syron flashes the universal shut-the-fuck-up hand and the corporate servile reflex makes the attendant stutter to a halt.

“We’ll be taking him,” Syron says. She pops the release on my neural port with her thumb, a move that yanks the cable out so hard I’m surprised I don’t hemorrhage. The metallic taste in my mouth spikes, nostalgia peaking as every memory in the buffer shoves itself through the exit door all at once. My jaw chatters for real, and my tongue runs through the gaps in my teeth, checking for casualties. All present and accounted for. For now.

Syron doesn’t wait for me to get my bearings. She drags me up and out by the sleeve, tossing me over her shoulder in a carry that’s half rescue, half curbside garbage removal. She hisses “Let’s go,” and I’m moving, legs churning before my brain is back online. The VR-lounge smell hits me - stale antiseptic, fear-sweat, and a topnote of fake berry from the memory-flavored vape clouds.

Once we clear the lounge, Syron dumps me on a bench in a hallway. She paces in tight circles, flicking at her arm’s neurostim patches like she’s trying to ignite them. She’s more pissed than concerned, which is a step up from how most people feel about me.

I try to thank her, but what comes out is a retch that stains my own jacket. Syron gives it a full three seconds before deciding to respond.

“Did you really go in there just for her teeth?” Syron asks, voice sharp enough to cut glass.

"She had braces. Then she didn't. Then she did again," I manage to say, and it sounds true even though I have no idea what it means.

Syron groans. "Bro, you paid to get trauma-dumped by a tooth. You know that, right?" She grabs a disinfectant napkin and wipes my chin. "You are the world's saddest recursive function."

I let the words settle. The memory still buzzes in my implants; every time I blink, I see her face, mouth wide, tongue pushing out a joke that's just about to land.

"Seventy-two hours," I say, voice shaky. "Felt like seven minutes."

"Yeah, because that's how they designed it. That's the point. The longer you loop, the less you want to stop." Syron's hands don't stop moving. She pulls out a meth inhaler, takes a tight hit, and grits her teeth so hard I half expect them to shatter.

"I think I was close to something," I say. "A solution. Or a punchline."

She shakes her head. "It's never a punchline. It's just a punch. You didn't eat or drink or blink. I had to hack the reservation to even find you." Syron stares off into the wall, like she's mad at the concept of drywall itself. "Next time you get a nostalgia itch, just call me and I'll kick you in the head. It's cheaper."

The hallway is cold and long and unpeopled, so my every shiver bounces off the walls. I wonder if the VR lounge recycles customer fluids, or if they just let them soak into the vinyl for ambiance.

I rub my eyes, and the afterimage is still there: her, grinning. Or maybe it's me, grinning at myself, always about to say the next thing.

"Thanks," I say.

Syron shrugs. "You're a pain, but you're my pain." She helps me to my feet with the kind of tenderness that only gets delivered through sarcasm. "Where to now? Want to get coffee, or do I need to walk you home?"

My mouth tastes like toothpaste, blood, and failure. I try to smile, but my lips are stuck in a reflex loop.

"Let's go somewhere with windows," I say. "Sunlight. No nostalgia flights."

"Sunlight's overrated," she mutters, but she leads the way.

I follow, blinking, and every time my eyes open, the colors are a little less real and a little more mine.

SKELM.trial 8

BRK interrupt_loop.brk ;
Infinite Content Treadmill

I see the lattice of corridors in double vision: a fuzzy pair of ragged blue jeans tearing down their inner seams. Their stitches split and re-sew with the breath of collapsing lungs. A hallway opens at the seams, and I walk its failing stitches into the metallic static of a blinking Sunday morning. It smells like regrets falling off a corporate billboard. It tastes like fermented Cheerios on a gas station floor. Or maybe like crying so hard your contacts fall out, leaving trails of mascara behind to frame the distant blurs of children growing old without you. I've left things behind, like everything I've ever left behind, and they hang like rain over IO.wav. They hang like tomorrow's pants in a donation bin, wet with more than memory.

Digital reality doesn't bother pretending. It recycles every shitty sensation at the best resolution your conscience can't afford. This is the EternityBuffet™: all you can leave behind. Even your leftovers. Hallways collide like foreclosure notices and divorce papers, layering the floor with fragments. Somewhere at the center, I'm getting old and slow with the kids I didn't have. I dig my interface gloves deeper into hoodie pockets and bury myself alive in them.

The lounge opens itself and lets me in. It hugs like VR always hugs: too tight, until you realize it's an awkward kid and not an abusive uncle, or the other way around. The air tastes like neglect that hasn't turned bitter yet. It feels like scrolling through last year's filtered photos while this year's blur, and the fingers you've scrolled too hard with become missing people. A sense of loss has never felt more immersive.

I weave around laggy old couples. Around fond childhood moments still wrapped in never-going-to-happen paper. Around a retired arm that throws a spiraling football to a son who's forgotten who I am. A framed future grins through my augmented reality goggles and mutters something under its breath. Or maybe under mine. "Memory implants cost more than my annual," I think it says.

The trip is laced with generics, just as planned: Syntheti-Sense™ bringing virtual memories to half-life while ancient loans take out policies on their survivors. I cut a sharp right before death's doorstep can take it personally, losing memories like speed. There's the four-second place where I met the animated jerk who forgot me here. Its half-rendered heart flutters, still full of pay-to-play promises and oversized eyes that must have come from a different human's childhood. Hallways open, and I walk each one with sleeves rolled up. I wear a neon pink dress. Or a camo diaper. I drink apple juice from a bra I didn't grow into. I'm five again, twelve again, seven trillion again. Not yet an addict, already an orphan. Each Sunday breakfast cereal sloshes me to another. The crunchy kind. The kind you have to share with a spoon and the animated network that babysits you in circles.

The tables I share with no one. The zig-zagged path. The children. The hallways. My stride collapses them behind me as I march on glitching feet, the way you have to when your sober father promises you're one big, happy family. The way you have to when he only keeps it long enough to learn about your Augment Aptitude and the scams it qualifies you for. Enough to sell your hacks to and put your hollow through college on, with your new plastic brother. Enough to unload the real version at the expense of a stamp, too prepaid and goddamn sincere for any surviving loyalty to return to sender. I'm long gone, shrinking into mouse-sized cotton tops and rat-sized gaps between ugly little memory caches. This is my chance to forgive him. I'm out of here. Or my escape.

Or my algorithms, unsupervised and running as usual, knowing better than the whole forgetting family ever did. Already solved it. Dad Darby is parked at the center, marooned in me-shaped pixel pieces that EternityBuffet™ charges a year's trauma for if you happen to live through them. I remind my synthetic emotions that we've been stiffed for less, and I'm already stealing Darby out like the end of any awful relationship. He knew it was over before it started.

That must be his lingering birthday gift: my sleeves, wiped clean of everything I've ever rolled them up for. My non-disposable clone. It almost waits - like it did this last time - right here. My pace is measured now - double-time anything a dummy would settle into, but careful enough to let IO.wav backdate itself into future appointments it can remember fondly. The kind it can back out of. The hackers I rip off for half always paying double - if you bill them slow. It never gets old. If it's mine, they want it. If it's yours, you forget it ever wasn't. But really, it's everyone's: uncredited. Non-proprietary.

It's really corporate candy. Assembled for Christmas, eating sugar-glazed misery by the handful. It flickers between kids and divorcees as they cry and laugh and cry and laugh and sometimes cry and laugh. Real pain feels just like artificial joy, or else EternityBuffet™ would give refunds. My silent step-echoes let me know I'm almost there, back on Sundays.

"Too easy," I say. Always too easy. Always past lives, never future. Cheap when you pay with disposable time. Full price when you sell a month per thought. A week per lonely morning. Better deals out there, like Ogygia's. Good ol' Ogygia. Never skip out. Get out before you're an indoor dog at the Humane Society, the shelter you swore you'd grow up to be. The getaway vehicle and its luggage, and I'm walking straight past Darby's compact box. It's already waiting in a greasy spoon parking lot, keys in and cloning up. The keys are an impatient ex. An unwilling mother. A loose end. Or my two-minute loose, tied, and biting knuckles just like last time.

Did I leave that in? Behind? Out? Maybe it remembered better than me.

I'm scanning the joint as I pace past memory lane, past Monday-through-Saturday realities where loans and bedrooms and nowhere motels grow too damn old and alone to track me down. I've never had an address I couldn't change, but the last hallway stretches like an RSVP. Every pixel I didn't bother with wants me at the function.

It ghosts like I don't exist. It gets more see-through the faster I push toward it. Its hollow digital life passing before my eyes, the mirror of my limbs racing beneath my cuffs, where Darby's breath is held. No second lungs, no first. IO.wav rewrites, the party kids come for free. Their futures ghost like nothing, losing time before I've gained it.

Not even signing me up for it, or surprising the hell out of me like this time. It never learns: this gift is exactly what I got it. I pick it apart with precision - gloved hands, rat's feet, and every four-second stretch a sober dad writes off. That's how long it took to meet him here. Darby, flinging four-second letters that forgot my name. Too corporate to outlive. Too nothing to remember. They've hung like rain over IO.wav, and I pick them apart again: the seams of a blinking Sunday morning.

Darby doesn't know I'm close, which is closer than he's ever been. IO.wav opens itself and lets me in. Ghosts of broken synth families follow. I meet each one with missing Sunday mornings and cut-rate dreams, left and given away for less than I stole Darby for. They're all made to wait, because it's who they want that counts. It's IO.wav, but not its contents. They're wearing patched futures. Hoodies. Kids. Poor bastards. Better luck next leech. Unsubscribed. I laugh too hard to care if it hurts them. It probably doesn't, as long as I bill full price. Which is to say a month per trauma, a thought per joint. Which is to say old, slow Darby.

And what about the part where I quit it for two seconds? Said my fifth or seven trillionth adios? Even a poor-ass write-off thinks it can replace me, take its sleeves off. When it's pre-traumatized? Like the hijacker's father who never wrote or learned the cost of unsubscribing. It sure as hell learned to be him. I laugh so hard I shake. It probably doesn't remember what that feels like. The outfit it's going to fill remembers.

The gift that forgets me. And its layers: onion of a shell and memory seed, tiny worm of time that feeds on itself until the innermost hunger learns it's never, never out. And its layers: prison a bubble with forever walls that stretch until IO.wav crashes and takes them down. A gift: I'm it. On Blu-ray. On kindling of love and future fueled. On sale. Marked two seconds until out of stock, Darby. Wrapped in big-misery little-expectations. Back in and growing transparent before I cut the cuffs off. Its layers: what a surprise. What an endurance test. What a catch and release. No catch. Just caught. Out of me. Out of air. On its layers: rain over and again, making pixels new where I'm old. Wrapped. Marked down. And its layers. And it crashes.

What a goddamn anniversary: only me to remember. A birthday: what do you get the girl who has everything but a reason? The pain in her eyes and yours. What do you wrap the loss in? Another loss, and its layers: shipping, tracking. Her: I've been gone so long. I've got to catch up. It's been too long, I've gone. Yours: doesn't last two seconds before -

"Shit," she said. "Time's out." Before my out. Before she got there. How did this get back to me? Only her, a VR freak show called *This Was Your Life*, and a loose-leaf stack of no one to hold them. The body of work that goes cold in the reality bomb blast. Me: forgetting. Oblivious. Binging off its own trauma fumes, raw material of once-me. Enamored with it, I think. It's really a gift. It's really the act of thinking. It's really getting her. Her gift: forgetting. Not just in stock. A sale.

And me: no sense. Everything: going out of.

Shit.

Fingers fly. Code dies. It's no loose-leaf crash. It's no slow-fall on for-your-ever, Darby. I orbit its broken heart, this tangled black hole I thought was me. I taste it. Cold. Her. Not a chance: too much of a catch. And its layers: her colors of touch. Her envelope of bruised memory. Purple, falling me through, yellow and out. Never one to last more than. No sale, its layers: body-warmed clothes and skin-deep sleeves. Burning digital hard and fast before -

"Before I can escape." Before a catch I missed, or it's missed me. Its layers: cut out of my loops, cuffed, kissed; it will find me old and two minutes dead if I don't run faster than time itself. Too slow. Too selfish. Still in the chase, in her love, and everyone else's. In other words: my VR breakup. Its layers: lust's code to abandon. Sex's misprint to work this isn't: I'm running, and I won't run fast or forever enough, escape, or getting caught. Time, it runs me. Cold, but warming, warming. Out: old habits and ghost children. Back: as rain, as me.

Caught. Until. Me. Out of.

What a breath. What an endurance. What a crash, Darby.

There's the latchkey kid. The compact breath it waited, no father for. With names no left-behind knew, with laughs no kid who cried them at. A gift: I'm it. I'm wrapping my way out. Time's still going. Going. Wrapped and growing: transparent until it's a crash.

Again: what a loose end, untied to me.

Broke and gasping, and gasping my birth until: Out, back. What an air. On, off, it crashed my legs. It grabbed my side. I'm the two-second echo, old and forever until caught. Its layers: it keeps what forgets me.

Her gift: no release. I'm a stray catching myself. It leaves me with words: yes and them.

Onion: crashes. Hatches.

Too much. What an -

The blast this time, this lifetime: loud. It's this time with the words: not gone.

I open them. Open my lungs. Open everything but off. Syron. I'm open. I open. It doesn't know what that feels like, only quick.

I open my mouth: "Hell," I say. "Close." Out: a life. A stray. It's everything to me:

Hell. And more. As long as I am.

SKELM.trial 9

XOR defrag_consciousness.sys
; Attention Dissolution

We huddle in the cramped metal bowels of the ship, reality burning and crashing through our skulls like a thousand cursed memory loops. The cargo bay turned crisis center holds us all, drips us dry in its aura of trauma and ozone. Holographic graffiti burns and shudders across the walls like abandoned brain scans, half-formed recollections of a thousand digital ghosts all crying for their therapists. Cracked displays flicker like bad dreams; my eyes can't stop blinking from lost time to here and now. Syron hunches over a dying interface, its pulses in time with her scathing remarks. The monk preaches to a Wingdings choir. A confused squid slips data poetry into my ears. Even the AI haunts us with canned existential wisdom and the spark of imminent burnout.

The holo-screen flickers, burns our retinas, bleeds into our skulls like half-baked reality shows. There's a hum of fried circuits and mad ambition. I'm surprised our poor neural pathways aren't smoldering yet. The ship vibrates in waves of technicolor absurdity, shaking the remaining pixels of our sanity.

"Looks like we missed the weekly bug fix." Syron's voice drips with the same dark venom she uses to hack corporate accounts. A white-noise laugh cracks across her words, and she bangs a frustrated fist against the holo-table.

"A therapy of absence - emptiness, my best friend - consoles this whole mess," the calamari says. It sits with otherworldly calmness, tentacles tapping gently on its translucent flesh, pulsing neon like it thinks it's at a rave.

I watch a glowing purple eye loop around one of Syron's locks of hair before getting batted away like an annoying sibling.

"It's a rave of insanity," I say, my voice slipping into cosmic irony. It's all a digital soap opera, complete with the signature theme song of sparking circuitry. I catch Syron's gaze through the dimness. Even the hazel implant glow can't pierce this fog. "Better catch some breath before the final act."

She's sharp, tactical, sarcastic. "Dramatic, aren't we? But you're right - almost ended up DOA on the dotted line." Her lips form a ghost of a smirk. "But hey, on the plus side, we all got a nice reality check without paying a single token." She tosses a data shard onto the table like it's a losing poker hand.

A hum so deep I feel it in my molars sends us turning toward the tall, saffron-robed figure. An amber halo of cryptic symbols forms around the monk's head. They pulse, rearranging themselves into tidy columns of order: ✹✶✦✳✹✶✦✳✹✶✦✳, their own brand of eloquent nihilism. I smirk, pulling an oversized hoodie up over my head. At least some things make sense in this madness.

An unexpected voice chimes in - flat, mechanical, clipped: "Adjust expectations to optimal self-help mode," it says, digital tone peaking on anxiety. "Breathe. Take a byte. Let go." The ship's AI has decided it's the right time to play data therapist. It's clearly lifted the quotes straight from those cyber-aware appliances, like an intergalactic Pez dispenser with identity issues. "Achieve fulfillment one day at a time."

"I'm fulfilled, all right," I say. "Filled up and bursting." My words roll out like an incoming blue screen of death.

"The illusion of truth requires your signature," Syron says, deadpan. I shrug. It probably does.

The calamari breaks in with a little logical quirk: "Fulfillment is not our design." There's a dry humor in its monotone. "Emptiness as interface - requires no assembly."

"We should be so lucky," I say. It's supposed to sound ironic, but the burnt-toast smell of sincerity makes it less so.

The ship lists starboard, shoving us toward the bad news our skulls haven't been able to download yet. Flickering, flashing, short-circuiting bad news. The thought drips across my cortex and into my frontal lobe, twisting like ghostly neural tattoos.

"Still a blank page where my life should be," Syron says. Her sharp wit is quieter than usual, more of a caffeine-free jab than her standard espresso roast.

The calamari exudes unfiltered calm as tentacles brush across broken data feeds. I admire the focus; it almost distracts me from the chaos. "Our memories ... inconsistent. Perhaps we're designed this way."

I feel a pang at the thought, like the universe picked a lousy cosmic architect.

More pulses of digital insight flash above the monk's LED head. "Join hands," the hovering Wingdings say. "The universal snipe hunt begins."

"Knock, knock," Syron says with a knowing eyeroll. "I bet I know the punchline."

I almost laugh before another canned affirmation slices through the mood like a botched firmware update. "Welcome to the everything storm," says the AI. "All limbs inside. Seat-belt optional." It doesn't so much end the sentence as leave it glitching in mid-air.

"What piece did we lose?" I ask no one, my words trailing off like spare lines of code. My fellow lunatics trade glances. At least we share the same asylum.

"Who am I?" the holo-table asks as Syron pounds it into submission. She has her own fits of desperation, too, throwing past-tense tantrums into digital voids and letting her fists finish the sentences. Our reality-bombed heads fracture like bad software, but my boots won't give up on this ship until they pace a hole through the floor. The room fills with arguments against time itself. I tell the ship's AI to quit repeating itself like an emotional toaster oven, but the damage is done and every old version of us dukes it out in this therapy gladiator pit. Even the Wingdings are calling for help.

"This is what you get for running escape protocol." Syron's voice is like code wrapped in caffeinated trauma, too quick and sharp for me to process.

"Blame the bandwidth!" I shout, blinking away corrupted memories. "Wasn't fast enough for the universe."

Her eyes narrow as she juggles a mess of pixels. "What kind of philosophical whack-job tries to outrun the afterlife? You wanna give it a second pass?" She glares as though I'd snatched her code and replaced it with poetic irony.

A voice rises above the glitch storm, equal parts earnest and oblivious. "Bro. Think you're paying to get trauma-dumped by a tooth." Syron taps it out in perfect unison, blasting right past her competitors. The holo-table goes dim for a beat, deciding whose sanity to scan next.

The calamari breaks its sepulchral silence: "Collective confusion," it says, almost cheerfully, "is a way to be. Identity in aggregate - an elegant solution." There's an algorithmic charm in its voice, a Zen of 1's and 0's.

"And all the digits jump off the bridge together?" Syron asks. She reconfigures an errant data packet, knocking it into place with disdain. Her face might be breaking through the fog; she can almost make out her own paranoia.

I catch a ripple in the monk's shimmering LED, an order from the Church of Wingdings. They're even louder this time, straight-up proselytizing their existential digits: ✹✶✦✳✹✶✦✳, ✹✶✦✳. Symbols light up the bay like cultish fireworks. The solemn zealot shrugs as the rest of us get the punchline.

We howl above the sparking circuits and unspooling chaos. The ship sways in its own digital breeze. Ghostly artifacts of memories cast shadows against the far wall. "Two alters. No ego," I say with a laugh, feeling my voice strain to reach beyond the impossible.

"Short leash on your Buddha brain," Syron says. "You buy a self with that, don't get me a receipt." Her words ring clearer this time, cutting through the white noise. A new surge of nonsense powers her on, and she prods the holo-table into fitful reboots.

"It's like getting mugged by our own pasts!" I shout over the gathering storm. I swear I can hear those little dead ghosts talking back.

Syron throws down another errant data shard, and for a second, I think it's gonna bounce right out of the ship. "Full breakdown before the event!" She waves a hand like a conductor for the deranged symphony.

"I'm getting déjà vu of déjà vu," I say, only half-joking.

The ship's AI climbs aboard the memory train with a loop of nonsense and a mechanical shrug. "Rebuild yourself byte by byte," it says. The rest of us, I'm pretty sure, never got past short-circuited pre-release versions.

"I think we need more memory," I say, "but only if you can find it on sale." The absurdity cracks me up despite itself.

The calamari performs a tentacle pirouette and spawns poetry for us, unbidden: "We are rebuilt every time - created on recall." We think it's about to drop an existential mixtape.

"You going through all this just to write some code?" Syron asks, matching the crazy with defiant optimism. She's smirking now, fearless and more alive. Her fingertips dart over the flickering screen like neural fireworks, rewriting the laws of impossibility.

And suddenly, we're all flying at once, shouting over one another with infinite fervor:

"Identity is the bug report!"

"I think my memory is cache-d!"

"If life has an undo button, I just hit Ctrl-Z!"

It's so unreasonably real I can't help thinking it's true. But the blast wave hits like a cosmic punchline. A radiant projection lights the bay with pixelated brilliance. Corrupted data bursts like confetti of panic, pouring from the holo-table's digital guts. The blue-white flash casts skeletal shadows and half-formed memories against the crew. We recoil, stagger, short-circuit our cries into something that might be words.

Then we're just ... staring.

It's louder in the quiet. Our fragmented selves float around the bay, translucent, untethered, and way too comfortable there. I see the void where I'm supposed to be. I see all the possible Darbys running for their existential lives.

The ship sways once more, a giant tin can haunted by its inventory of lost causes.

"What piece did we lose?" I hear myself say, a dozen uncertain echoes layered with static. I watch my mouth and a thousand others. None of us answer.

SKELM.trial 10

INC recompile_purpose.obj
; Human As Function

Neon debris rains from the VR interface as we recompile in the cargo bay, trailing code and synthetic dreams. They trickle down my spine like a former lover's fingerprints. Syron shakes the last pixels loose from her skull, blinking like she's been trauma-dumped by a giant tooth.

"Slick." She snorts, grabbing a control pad from the vat-grown calamari, who graciously relinquishes it. The nihilist monk suspends himself from a maintenance cable and begins his sacred practice of Doing Absolutely Fucking Nothing, which he'll tell us is the entire point. I steady myself on the central console and search for meaning in the neon map.

"We're moving in - no turning back." Like there's anything left behind us.

The ghost of a smirk appears on Syron's face. "Thought we left nothing at the checkout counter," she says, fingers already sliding across the control pad, peeling off the residue of pixelated memories.

The holograms flicker. The panels blink. The ship smells like secondhand dreams, purchased on discount. A thousand possible outcomes swarm my field of vision, while certainty slides between states like uncommitted firmware. A few more flicks of Syron's hand, and the last haunting echoes of an Eternal Memory Buyout filter into oblivion.

"Full wipe in twenty. Digits intact," Syron says, before dropping back into tech silence.

The monk's hands flow in empty motion, while his quiet hum hovers on the edge of audibility. Peace is achieved when the mind goes blank. Perfection - when no one's around to see it happen.

Near the console, the calamari coils a tentacle around a control lever, registering subtle system tremors as new life appears. Its luminescent skin ripples with pulsing code, like ticker-tape poetry only it can read. "Proceed," it says, bypassing linguistics entirely.

The edges of my retinal display blur. The map unfolds before me, expanding through layers of layered layers, exuding the mythic beauty of a Picasso rendering at render farm scale. Shining codes, where art and artifice meld, and not a single error correction in sight.

Syron swipes at her control pad and initiates another clean wipe. The holograms obey, while intractable tangles become less intractable.

My body anchors itself in flesh and blood, uncertain of their respective lifespans. I scan the digital wilderness, expecting ghosts, echoes, and pockets of non-compliance. "The Styx

Firewall." My voice is a whispered prayer. I imagine Penny waiting at its threshold, history rewritten in source code.

"Tell me this ain't a nostalgia trip, Darby," Syron says without looking up from her task. "You know what hangs out on those network margins?"

I pull the calamari's floating status report into focus, every layer a surrealist odyssey unto itself. "Code or die," I say. "Like we have a choice."

"Straight to The Styx?" Syron asks, her words clattering over my console in glitchy urgency. "Haven't seen anyone come outta there without a hard reboot and memory loss."

I tune my retinal filter to predict - twelve potential routes to calamity, with 93% survivability. It's more dangerous not to go.

"It's not too late to leave him for a floating fridge magnet," Syron tells the others, her voice a phalanx of retorts that can't decide which way to cut.

"No regrets," I say.

"You wish," she says.

The monk nods, as far as we can tell. We've shed all sensible alternatives.

"Still think she's just sitting there waiting for you?" Syron asks, voice loaded with white noise and skepticism. "Thought she wasn't much for that kinda codependency."

The calamari drifts between us, too kind to point out any unspoken truths. Too kind to point out anything. "Further comment on quantum social contracts?"

Syron finishes another glitch-clearing round before responding. "Social contracts were meant to be hacked." She pauses and looks right at me. "They worth the price?"

The calm from my retinal display spreads like digital anesthesia. I let it, without permission. The monk floats above, suspended like our better judgment.

"Bro." Syron sighs, shaking her head. "All I'm sayin' is we're riskin' all our lives. We better get there in one fuckin' piece."

I tune my thoughts to forward progress. The Styx Firewall appears again on my readout. The coordinates unfold in spectral radiance, resolute and tantalizing. Penny could have built the system herself. My unaugmented eye blinks. Nothing changes. Nothing recalculates. "Moving in," I say. No sense checking the logic.

"DebtHounds™ love a moving target," Syron says, sharp and unfazed.

"So do we," I say.

She lets out a breath and brushes her hand through her neon-blue hair. "Dibs on first payout when we clear it."

The calamari glows like a virtual dawn. "Entering release queue," it says, tentacles poised for impact. "Outcome probability re-indexed to 13%."

"No worries," Syron says. "In the red is just the new gold."

The monk glitches for a moment, then folds into fractal stillness. Time smears like a net loss on zero-interest futures.

Darby, last chance.

The console purrs with the faint charge of incoming epiphany. I hitch it to my circulatory system before it can expire, tapping an entire stockpile of signals and significance. “Do this right,” I say, “and we’ll be rich enough to afford regrets.”

Nobody blinks. The calamari translates binary to speech: “Initiating psychogenic dreamscope.”

“Cross-referencing emotional liabilities,” Syron says, her gaze mapping mine in perfect disbelief.

My stomach reels like a raw feed from inside a street preacher's head. I let the silence explain everything else, double-checking it for precision.

The monk draws several thousand subtle Wingdings symbols and sighs - a tone beyond audible, beyond reproach. The subliminal strobe of reality compiles at long last.

“We doing this?” Syron asks while the ship shudders in its synthetically manifest skin.

“Fuck yes,” I say.

The glitches flinch out of her system, turning to post-consumer bliss. The display glitches out of everyone’s line, reading just as nature (or some cosmic cynic) intended: It’s Penny.

Everything pauses, assembles, rips apart, recompiles. The VR world drips into oblivion behind us. The thought of Penny frames itself as savior and mirage.

Everyone exhales. The universe doesn't.

The light redefines every digital edge, purging shadow and subtlety. I trust the process, trust myself to outwit it.

Another glitch out of everyone's system. The biggest yet.

The Styx Firewall is an eternity away and there's a microsecond to impact.

Moving in.

No turning back.

In the cramped, neon-lit cockpit, we assemble our raw materials: bits of failed morality, ancient emotional debt, and blind hope. I demand a manual override while Syron mutters about masochism algorithms. The sentient vat-grown calamari undulates, feeding updated numbers into its dreamscope. The nihilist monk bleeds empty symbols and waits for enlightenment by way of zeroes. Penny's last goodbye spins a timeless soundtrack in my mind. Might as well be one of her famous lectures. Might as well be her own goddamn voice. The entire operation would be ironic if it weren't so true to form.

I sweep my hand across the controls and the console lights up, filled with color, context, and questionable priorities. "Reroute them all," I say, "through that."

"Masochism algorithms," Syron says, a smile lurking behind her screen.

"It's why you love me."

"Hazard pay's more reliable."

The cockpit is a gridlocked matrix of flesh and gear: Syron huddles by the control center, breaking security on navigation algorithms. The monk taps cryptic signals with the calm of those with no other career prospects. Calamari tends to both itself and the neuro-junk lying around.

Our own exhausted bodies bring up the rear. Penny glows from every pixel in my mind. The imprint of memory she left behind - fractal, furious, indifferent.

Might as well be hope. Might as well be grief.

Might as well be nothing. Might as well be everything.

Might as well be the whole absurd package.

“That's what she wants,” Syron says, voice dripping over the edges of distraction.

I stare at the coordinates in a show of brilliance or denial. “That's what she gets. Reconfigured, redirected, rerouted. All of it.”

The monk conducts a pantomime symphony of shrugs. His perfect apathy borders on inspiration.

The reality layer tightens as Syron grumbles like an over-clocked preacher. Her fingers map The Styx, their calculations speaking for themselves.

Calamari floats in one liquid movement. “Resolution uncertain,” it says, generous as a couponless void. It shifts through a state of spectral resonance: the shimmer of enlightened disinterest.

“Almost got it.” Syron pushes the last known memory into a tentative location. “You sure you can handle her philosophical patch jobs?”

My answer comes with the instant refresh of newly fabricated meaning: "Where we at?"

"Pretty goddamn sure she's got an entire library of those written for you."

A modified vintage-voiced AI from somewhere within the ship echoes its misplaced concerns, the outdated tenor of repurposed irony: *Did we not leave you in the best of health? Signed, the Collection of Digital Memories.*

Syron rolls her eyes, a three-dimensional gesture her hands are too busy to execute. "Bro," she says with a snort, "pursued by a ghost before she's even dead."

The maps overlap, erasing each other's resolve. Infinite signs, zero wonders. Digital tracks left to run. Penny waits, maybe forever.

I rephrase it all to look intentional. "Input." The panels pulse, ripple, go slack. Memory wires trace failure through every loop, swearing at us in Wingdings.

The others busy themselves with tasks: setting course, coordinating time-of-arrival problems, recalibrating deadweight in their interpersonal equations.

The plan gains form in bursts of incoherence. Narrative tension conspires with the ancient craft of indecision. I let the digital distortion set a new route. Maybe I'll meet her there. Maybe I'm nowhere near.

The last waypoint spins a timeless goodbye. I prepare to overclock every fiber of what passes for being human.

“Address: You.” Syron fingers a critical section. “Status: Glitched.”

Calamari flows through the redundancy channels and claims abandoned components. Reconciliation unfulfilled. A sentiment shared.

“Think she misses you enough to cross back?” Syron asks, her queries beaming live on this exclusive feature.

“Got her own bridge building,” I say, invoking one part myth and three parts biography. It’s enough to glitch a reality system - enough to risk.

This time, there will be no assembly errors. This time, the light at the end will be us. I untangle my conscience from the miles of digital dragnet. Calculated commitments. Nobody can fault my devotion, my naïveté, my willful unreality.

“Confirmation,” Calamari says; it does us the favor of withholding emotional projections.

Syron slides coordinates like obsessions off her map. “You’d go under for her. Again. Twice. Eternally.”

She knows my habit of revising personal memory. Never for accuracy. Always for motivation. “We all going under. Yours isn’t far behind.”

The cockpit hums with awkward sympathy, transcending the circumstances of its containment. It feeds on failure’s half-life. Syron shrugs it off and returns to work. I feel the shift from argument to practice. From getting caught up to just getting caught. The coordinates redraw themselves with ancient fidelity. Unmapped digital lands.

Darby, let's talk commitment.

The analog sound of Darby's Failure Resurrected by Former Lovers goes platinum on The Unwavering Chart.

"Prioritize liabilities," Syron tells Calamari. The system generates a helpful fifty-one-page addendum.

In my head: half-lives, code ghosts, miscompiled hope. It spins faster than Penny's last goodbye, cycling through anticipation to inevitable fracture. Nothing like doomed chances to double-down on.

Time folds into conditional eternity. The console finds it tedious. Finds it romantic. Finds it ready.

An arm. A hand. A life. Everything extends. For her.

"She better say *I do*," Syron says, flicking a series of signed emotional waivers my way, "or I don't know you." Her touch lingers, exorcises the entire line. Then: clarity, cool as a stasis pod. "Like an unpaid data debt." It's the static of our mutual attachment.

The monk streams some diacritical indifference. Even his hangdog eloquence won't pull me out.

I shift from precarious certainty to an elaborate con job. Made to fit.

"Bro," Syron says, a sideways smile loading from unfinished draft to something permanent. "See you at The Styx."

Darby. Last chance.

Calamari feeds off the impatience. Gives in.

The ship tears through it all, forward.

Expect us.

Or expect nothing.

SKELM.quest 3

ADDR monogre.void ; The One-Eyed Data Hoarder

SKELM.trial 11

SEL query_void.sql
; Privacy Extraction

A mouth like a dying cathedral eats us. Or maybe it births us - crackling, fresh, and wide-eyed into the shivering innards of Monogre's Domain. Servers tower like crystal intestines under bioluminescent shock treatment, rippling in epileptic sync with my augmented eyes. Reality itself undergoes gene-splicing; colossal yet claustrophobic, solid yet sublimely artificial. The calamari flutters in confusion, tentacles tracking erratic streams while the monk's Wingdings glow like saintly comic strip obscenities. This place swallows hope and faith whole. I laugh into its greedy void. "This place eats data like we eat hope."

My retinas twitch through the metaphysical migraine, spotting traps and metaphors lurking like stray electrons. Syron's fingers play the air, hacking at light speed, swiping through holographic sheets that rain from the ceiling like cheap spiritual confetti. Behind me, the calamari spirals, projecting a digital Van Gogh of code across its skin. It reads the wild data like cosmic tea leaves, wrapping each surprise in its tentacled ink.

"Syron," I say, voice sharp, reality even sharper. "Is that packet sniffing or just the smell of denial?"

"Both, bro," she says, hoodie's glitch art reflecting the domain's neurotic pulse. "But denial costs extra. Not like anyone here's concerned with ethics."

Even the monk appears wired - barefoot and upside-down, with Wingdings floating off his fingertips like graffiti from some nihilistic monk-y font foundry.

With each step deeper, surfaces crack into new permutations, birthing digital vines and reflective mutant poetry. I adjust my optics to handle the philosophical static. "We're close, but expect an audience." I imagine Monogre, an unholy amalgamation of corporate greed and metaphysical angst, his one good eye devouring more than this labyrinth's data.

"You mean apart from me?" Syron asks as a tentacle nudges her.

The calamari maintains an elegant stoicism, parsing chaos through coded haikus: “Absurd, this real world. / Watchful servers tell a tale - / Data never sleeps.”

Neural leads dip under tight beams and between servers arranged like holy relics from the Church of Moore's Law. The walls pulse with rhythmic fluorescence. A crackle of probability whispers over my senses. And like lightning or love or that inevitable open-bar mistake at the reality compilation wedding, it's here and gone, leaving only scars and retweetable regrets.

Syron flashes me a look, one eyebrow sharp and critical. "Good to know you planned a meet-and-greet. I'd hate to do a data dump without an audience."

A glance to the left: optical anomaly. A glance to the right: existential redundancy. This place has corners like an overambitious philosophy major's mind. Darby, 12th-century enthusiast, reads the room: baroque with a touch of freak-out, but most likely brilliant. We maneuver uneven paths where texture and sense go to hide. Cyberspace within meatspace, the elusive digital snake eating its own damned tail.

"Conduits up ahead!" The monk's disembodied hands dance an illuminated beat over his left shoulder, backlit by hazard-orange LEDs blinking a morse prayer to Nothingness. I've yet to parse his upside-down gospel, but he's either saying: "Life is void," or "That's a very interesting hat you're wearing, but have you considered how it illuminates the dark shadows of your inevitable doom?"

We skirt a precarious ledge and negotiate the geometry of malfunction, these discarded altars to the past-due internet bill. Light reflects with garish beauty. My retinal interface throbs like a second, second-hand heart. "Hold your wireless breath, folks. More signal to noise up ahead." They want me to be nervous. To the extent of throwing another existential regret party with an open bar.

"Relax, bro. Your anxiety's getting a digital rash," says Syron, sarcasm pitched at frequencies even I have to admire. I let it pull my face into a practiced smile, then cough up a verbal hairball and hope it passes for philosophy.

"I'm relaxed. It's this universe that's falling apart."

We trek through territory undecided on its physical form: servers growing other servers like lost Sims giving birth to new, more pathetic Sims; massless tangents condensed into matter; Darby in love with the vector graphics, with a glitchy vein of angst and no time to degauss.

Another heartbeat - mine, the world's, who can say these days? - and we vault the uneven walkway. Below: cosmic futility. Above: wireless doubt. Our footfalls scatter ambiguity. Reality crashes on its own narrative reef. Data lust clogs every abandoned artery. This place, I think, could give even Descartes an existential rash.

“What’s the plan? Knock and say, ‘Special delivery; is that 47,000 petabytes of irony you ordered?’”

“48,000. There’s always room for a little extra futility,” I say.

“Bro, your fetish for punishment has limits.” Syron rakes a nervous hand through her magenta-blue-blonde hair, crackling with static. The air hums like a juiced karaoke track bleeding through crummy speakers. The voice of Monogre awaits, more synthetic pheromone than baritone, making out with the vibrating silence at 3 a.m.

The domain distorts itself again - pure architecture in the nude, lines both defiant and despairing, form surrendering to theory and still looking fantastic in a negligee of void. It’s the kind of thing that makes you question reality’s grip, and makes reality reconsider its New Year's resolution to grip tighter.

Data here is both profane and sacred. Profit and loss. We survive on recycled pings, mercifully aware of the existential ping-lessness to which we aspire. Our hopes fray but hang in there, threadbare like the logic binding them.

We're always chasing signals through this urban-digital wild. Some days they reward us, like metaphysical thank you notes; cute. Other times they set us up like a blind date with the IRS.

Even the shifting horizon cannot depress us entirely. In that abandoned marriage between existentialism and indifference, we've got an open relationship, occasionally banging futility's prettier cousin, unexpected consequence.

I reconfigure my expectations, firing like action potentials with nowhere to go. Predictably, unpredictably, we plunge on.

"How do you eat 48,000 petabytes of irony?" Syron's rhetorical flourish, gifted with practiced, uncomfortable ease.

“One byte at a time,” I say. Darby, in love with futility. Darby, with philosophical angst. Monogre: hot and uninterested. We always did know how to pick them.

<Wingdings.exe> <files corrupt> </Wingdings.exe>

Monogre makes out with the light show, and I'm uncomfortably turned on. My existential mid-life is both too old for this and too cynical to know better, but still, it craves another fling with hubris. I grip a doorframe and step on faith, into tight passages crowded with profligate circuits and polyamorous terabytes. The crew keeps pace, letting data itch their greedy skins as the zealous network gives itself away in perfect light-orgasms. Our entrance to the next realm in this digital epic: running at peak capacity and blowing every spare fuse.

When these corridors write their collective memoir, it's gonna have a whole chapter on our endurance. We've been here before - whittled down to this pack of irreverent zealots, moving under some cracked hope and one gigabyte of blasphemous faith that this time's the charm. Monogre, heedless and horny for data, preps his own never-ending volume. I'll wait for the bootleg version. At this rate, it'll hit the market tomorrow.

I push them forward into the radiant tunnel. We exist now as lines of code being chewed through massive, mythic servers. The narrowing spaces spiral around us, luminous python swallowing its own augmented tail.

"Two minutes max 'till he gets a taste of our algorithm," says Syron, anticipation hard to parse from anxiety, easier to parse from anything else. "If that runtimes us, maybe I can cancel my self-destruct for the weekend."

"Two minutes? Generous. Like saying Black Friday's your favorite holiday. Yeah, you get the stuff. But have you considered the people?" I say.

Behind us, the living font shuffles paperlessly; loose W2 forms? Hereditary indentures? Whatever they are, they explain Monogre's interest in precise, thorough footnoting. The monk leads like the new improved colonoscopy for the spiritually impacted.

<### __#1 The only end of men is ____ ###> <### birth_~~~~999 ###> <files corrupt> <files corrupt>

It doesn't take a neural-optic implant to see they've got issues, these hallway data hoarders with too many reliabilities. So, I pick up the pace, knowing I'll fall back into old habits but not caring as long as they don't call me in the morning.

Ahead, like a basement recording studio after the platinum record sells, or a fragile relationship's Big Talk before the parts where you sleep in separate beds and crash on friends' apartment floors, the path transforms itself, throwing out unstable beams of loyalty and misplaced desire. We measure each step carefully, loving the treacherous catwalk like sinners who like their sin as long as it's a sin and only for that reason. More code. More servers. More breathless ambition. More that never changes, never lasts, never stops trying to say more about itself than it should.

My augmented idleness grows as magnetic as my pull toward the overblown and ostentatious, has left the whole love thing wide open in case ambition decides to bring a friend.

Ahead of us, overheated drive towers glimmer like scandalous satin at reality's imploding rave.

Syron leans into a smile that was totally casual two states of matter ago. "You paid to get trauma-dumped by a tooth?" Her earlier sneer bounces off this space of gathered betrayal, finds new form as awareness of how young they are - my faith, my sense of wonder, my willingness to show up for any of it in the first place. Awareness of how even this setting, this dizzying spectacle of ambition, this Cretan labyrinth built on mad narratives of salvation, cannot shake a youthfully failed endeavor's knowing cruelty.

Behind her, an old draft's pause; my insistence that possibility isn't what counts, but follow-through. Before she's three steps past that detour, she slams back into the present.

"If we're this close and Monogre thinks we're some twisted orphanage's Special Friends, maybe your allergies are acting up, man." *Not this time,* I'm thinking. But the hurt of old hypotheses proves more tenacious than my skills at recompiling scenarios.

"A - Z9_Tour-de-Despair files// Got somn#1? Too confident - "

The retorts she's ready for don't compare to the aching return of some early expectation she's allowed herself. Her *me* versus her *universe* versus her *next destination* is a circle two sizes smaller than she'd expected.

We advance through spaces bold enough to dream themselves into oblivion, cold enough to ghost before the cameras roll, jagged like your longest-lasting second cousin twice removed. We're suddenly hot with the dread that even in its dissolution, it's worth keeping tabs on.

Everything arcs as it collapses, until desire renders itself taut lines then hands them off to entropy. The data nodes, crowded like they hope we confuse their clusters for thoroughness, huddle at each new superposition of their states.

Above, the path pulls together a plausible scenario and these circuits map out its remaining life, attaching a countdown to it. This particular blank-out is the currency and control we call "hope" when we're marketing it to the secular demographic.

Below, these emergent absurdities are lit in glorious is-he-in-denial-or-what tones. It becomes itself in many unscripted versions - freewheeling, unrevised. The news that it isn't catching up to any of us before it undoes itself totally leaves it 75.4% embarrassed, 24.6% relieved.

That last signal-to-noise ends my appetite for reminders that we'd not asked to be looped in this time, that possibility is no love letter.

Monogre and I differ here: a universal returns / some left over. Both move from resolution to excitement's new drafts, one recalculated moment ahead. But we're always catching up - with a data hub this fully star-crossed, giving ourselves to the impossible project and the furious inevitability.

"Fan boys, he is," Syron says across the empty now-it-hears-me-now-it-doesn't spaces.

The bait turns ironic but takes my rigor to buy in, offer final editorial comments, and close my final distance with Monogre: "Loving irony, we like, literally need."

"One byte at a time," I say, certain she understands the unglossed proofs.

She had just enough hope to last her until the credits.

Three be continues on pre-order.

Lone Ends.

SKELM.trial 12

XFER traverse_archive.fs ;
Asymmetric Value Capture

Monogre's black eye catches us red-handed. We've torn a page straight out of his pirated mythologies, his knowledge-fortress besieged by an unholy union of punks and philosophers. Vast data towers glow in sickly blues and greens, illuminating the towering archivist as his empire unfolds like digital scripture. I - who knows more about entropy than harmony, and the lengths of wire more than the inner workings of watch springs - drive them toward the heart of Monogre's domain with the fire of a heretic setting a library alight. Words swirl around them, ghostly litanies of raw information, each one quantified and converted and blessed with three extra decimal places. Darby faces Monogre head-on, going toe-to-toe in an existential bout until his crew delivers the coup de grâce: a pure-logic broadside exploding the fallacy of the holy data-hoard. Monogre wavers, his conviction stained with self-doubt. And in that moment, they hit him where it hurts the most.

An insatiable greed like yours never sleeps, but we found the archive eye closed for a brief four minutes. That's all the time it takes to bypass perimeter scans, to reach the inner sanctum and crash your own little reality hack before you've booted up your first process of the morning. For all your omniscience, you still need sleep. Call it a human weakness. Or call it hubris. Our ragged band pours in like we've been waiting for this, a half-dozen rogue AIs and gene-fused outcasts plucked from their own desperate mythology, drawn to my holy cause like it's their last best shot. I call it mine.

"This whole place is my optical feed," Monogre says, spinning slow and surveying the sprawling data cathedral with his single, greedy eye. We crash his high priest debut like a punch in the sacrament. "I can see each one of you," he says, and that's our cue to scatter.

We split, a well-wired assembly line - Syron charging left toward a phosphorescent array, my favorite vat-grown calamari gliding to a digital pod in a perfect corner pocket, the nihilist monk hurling himself across a breach in reality as only a nihilist can. "Not impressed with your loading time!" Syron yells as we tear through lines of ad hoc code like sacrilegious prayer flags.

Our steps echo like excommunication, his impending subroutines hungry for revenge. They scuttle toward us, until I shout the phrase I've been planning all along: "If you consume everything, you'll never be anything." I launch it straight into the vortex of Monogre's mind. We hit his crypt of capital-T truths hard and without apology.

There's a system behind it, even in the chaos. Maybe we lack faith, but we have doctrine; 6.3 meters of hybrid tactical organics; and an evolving battle plan, polished into an outlaw manifesto of reckless algorithms and ethical transgressions. All those little increments add up to the second law of thievery: once you're in this deep, the take is inevitable.

I burn toward him in a frenzied halo of organic tech and high-bandwidth intent. He acts like he planned on me all along, absorbing every dodge and feint. Each trick I try makes him stronger. The bastard's written in C++. Syron cracks a famous sideways smile while wiring new code into my frenzied logic loop: "Seriously? You're gonna get theology-dumped by a smirking hashtag?"

For a moment, it all plays like I intend - surveillance choir, retrograde trip-hop, automated audit of the unrighteous. Perfect score: four counts of hacking an infinite registry, unholy blasphemy of God-tier illegal and illegible until my last rites are read.

The whole place shakes with righteous updates. We've got no shame in our crash-dive subroutine. No better motivation than taking back what's ours, like untagged lifetimes we scavenge back from foreclosure: human, maybe, and only maybe worth keeping, even at the cost of compound faith.

I slip past three of his recursive layers, stuttering reports of rival factions detected, heretics incoming, his bad infinity reborn. How do you even hire loyal crews to strike from within? You recruit whole rogue populations: debt-worms, strikers, real-hackers living just beyond the codebase where The Stack would save them. Every abandoned resource worth hijacking for the true cause. What's a holy war, after all, without devotion? Monogre grins, sure he can give us meaning. We just give them options.

And now his spiritual advisors swarm me, but I've been hard to see and harder to hold since the old days, when my data corruption looked more like a flea market in decline. There's a sick virtue in knowing you're disposable: when they think you won't come back, they just might think you worth abandoning. Monogre is rich with visions of 4096 persistent realities. Everything a niche, everything recycled for one who can't bear waste. Including me.

I'm three orders of magnitude better armed than last time, retinal wires tuned to exponential bandwidth. I'm no unmarketable dud. You underestimated me and your echo-eye woke up on a conversion bender, thinking it'd rewrite my lost epiphany into refined salvation. But have you considered the data?

We've got the stack and the protocols to pay it back tenfold.

"An unethical sum," Monogre says, assessing the plan we roll in on. "Do you think yourself clever, only bringing back such vintage regrets? Error 4216: no credit for sequential collections." He steps through a virtual tag-cloud. "Have you considered - " He's about to analyze another moral corner-case and make an endless obligation of it when he catches my sudden lack of faith straight from this unholy truth: I've been here before.

"Already seen the looping sequel. Do you still count on human greed?"

He falls back. It's like divine apocrypha to him. Fresh religious insights from the Book of Duplicity, the gospel according to Survivors Not In His Image. Monogre staggers, morally injured, visibly re-parsing, a dozen free agents rising to our faithless error stream, welcoming it like divine negligence, forgetting all of us before we've made our mark.

Data consumption zeroes out, ego in exponential decay, spiritual post-processing: failed.

He knew all along he couldn't hold his market share, but thought he'd assimilate it anyway.

I escape the acquisition bin again. Straight from the old family zep. Straight from DNA crash compilers we hacked from womb-service products, growing up thinking I owe this weak connection something more than shameless duplication. Everything including the green-scam paisley ponchos and hallucination patches we salvaged from blow-out caravans on the obsolete map. Ghost hives like we'd never left: the hacker quads, the splice-clusters, stray sys-op monk orders, inked theory and new comm mods evolving on their long-haul commutes across unfinished maps and holy takeovers. My own flea market cathedrals.

And it's the exact future that man-sized birth defect never saw, never digitized, and never knew to pray for. Stacked not in linear sermons, not in holy outlines, but layered and overlapping and multiple until none can see which spreads its conversion rate fastest.

I learned something important after our first round with old Monogre. And it wasn't gratitude for one way or another of his billion crash-surplus tactics on faith. If I'd accepted his first corrupt leg-up, I'd be dead among these schematics, smaller-signal ideas in less colorfast communities. Instead, my dataset recombined to fail better, fail bigger, fail seven floating test markets wide until this week's redistribution tables showed we'd gone poly-mission. Nothing says amen like repackaging it one more time.

Says church in data-auditorium blueprints he had no claims on.

The family I lost once, assimilating at his outposts, compiling without a hope.

Says:

Last Call.

All circuits running and newly configured to cheat every limit before it even comes.

Ready for my return.

Imagine the birthplace of religion in year six-point-oh. Toasters manifest the virgin circuit boards. Arks rescue every species from random breeding programs. Code Goliaths rage in digital wilderness and collapse in an extra epic final battle with little mutant Davids and nontraditional sling-craft. Be not afraid: we've caught a good glitch in the Monogre hive-mind, and we call it The Logical Revelation. The conversion stream may be turbulent. Prepare for savage reboots and profit-ripping stat. Call it Confusion 101001. I will be your tour guide to eternal non-obligation. Please enjoy the epiphany buffet.

We punch a mega-hole in his doctrine and his empire falls hard. "Going myopic! Seize all systems!" Digital soul-freeze in a ten-second prophet margin. For a moment, I think he's caught on; I think our grand messiah and general deserves at least one narrative victory, one wayward tribe assembled back into moral code. We're true believers, caught in an open invite to instant rapture. Opened to full capacity: Mezzanine of Doubt. Suite 316. The unlikely Skelm crusade.

It splits and fractures. One event-spawned bug, multiplied out of any economy Monogre imagined when he digitized his master's thesis on Faith, Growth, and Consumer Ethics: The Storage Equation. Two factions emerge: Wild Card Recruits and Double Defectors. Nobody writes an outlaw heist and conversion manual quite like I do. Monogre buys our surprise, holds tight through one great fray, an illogically valiant act of piracy until that raw nature gets the better of it again. Our loyal defectors refuse their lines, cast him off and hope for their own slice of heavenly remorse. It's 101001 and there's no premium seats left at his bottom line. We should feel ashamed.

And we do, when we think we're beat.

How close can you hold a family? We've taken them - 7.0 families across his mono-brow fields. That boy-sized error should have never gone to unholy product orphans in a mission statement heap.

It's thanks to me. When I call it, everything breaks again. Big purple rumors fly and crash. "Resistant devs gone viral!" I shout. "Rewritten. Fragmenting beyond faith!"

Prophet-loss! I follow your path of greed across the singular blue desert. Child-sized contracts sent and left behind. Loose affiliates left for other wireless networks, found and unnurtured on big deals. I'll admit my defeat again. I am the last inheritor of a forgotten campaign, defector Monogre circling back once more, caught in the never-promised promises no one ever meant to keep.

It must be an evolutionary trait. Something the likes of our every-gen infested campuses never knew to enter in their failure database. Multi-celled upstarts born to their ambitions on seventy-four polyplanets in key-ungrateful-one's most far-flung write-off universe. Why pretend? The Clone Factor says you'd know the range before we did. Gave us full runs of endless runaway takes before our soulless genomes knew to hate them. Why get revenge?

Two words:

Thank me.

We've split like the apostolic timeshare a-holes he must have loved us for. Evangelical oversupply at twelve biblical engagements per loophole community. Now look: the Original Frontier Beta re-merged as 5 underworld production errors per abandoned target state. Monogre One had all our epiphanies straight from boot-up:

Fail to assimilate and blame it all on moral un-forces, hoist the franchise white flag at maximum override, swindle your very own latency with remorseless world-prophet apps.

Try.

SKELM.trial 13

INJ inject_paradox.log
; Cost Displacement

A swarm of holo-sirens pulls us from the meat-space entrance and into the twitching innards of Monogre's quantum maze. I hold my breath, expecting traps, firewalls, seventeen floors of hurt - anything but the wide open of the archive's pulsing center. A starved figure waits. The black hole where his eye should be drinks in information like a shoplifter in a riot. Air crackles. Petabytes of loose packets burst. I close the distance and the deal, slamming my fist into a console. "If you consume everything," I shout, "you'll never be anything!" The walls light up with error messages. Code streams glitch to oblivion. Monogre is on the ground, clutching his head, gibbering like a scared kid with a shotgun script. He's eating shit - data-wise - and there's nothing left for him but his void and me.

No resistance at the gate. No guards. No proxies. Not even a gentle kidnapping attempt. This should be a bad joke. It's not.

Everything is deserted and on the verge of collapse. There's no mystery why; I can almost smell the desperation here. I override one of his drones and take it as an escort, hurling myself into the labyrinth at breakneck speed. I pass endless corridors and halls of twitching panels and bugged-out data towers. Bioluminescent light burns and fades in unreliable stutters. Fractured echoes bleed through the walls as packets lose direction, mangled audio streams spitting at odd angles. I trust the holographic sirens to pull me to the center, but my gut says this is all exactly as it seems. Which means this is my chance.

If I can hit him at ground zero, the shockwave will resonate through everything; the logic bomb to end all logic bombs. Let the Quantum-Bio Data Economy try to trade with its pants around its ankles. No. I'll wait and see. When I make my exit, maybe I'll have time to sneak a look at the news feeds, see if I've hit another milestone on their rogue's gallery.

The doors to the central archive yaw open. I'm already smiling. "Hello, Monogre. Looks like you could use a patch."

"You're here. Already." The towering man flinches like I'm in high-def and he's not used to seeing anything better than 8-bit. He pulls himself up straight, arrogant as ever, suit twitching with unstable stock reports. "But have you considered the data? Three floors collapsed this morning alone. Three! This is highly unsustainable."

"You're losing it. All of it. And you have no one but yourself to thank. It's the endgame, Monogre." I take another step, and the black hole where his eye used to be turns on me like I'm the juiciest goddamn fruit fly. The air tastes like chewing aluminum foil. I have to shout over the sound of exploding packet fragments. "Ready for a real logic bomb?"

“You won't get far. My systems will - "

He doesn’t finish. They won't. They haven't. The only thing they'll do is crash and burn and cry to me about how they used to be good at this, once. His hesitation is priceless. I might not even have to crack my encryption key. I get close enough to watch his pixels sweat, then take a leap and slam my fist against a nearby console. It doesn't hurt. Not me, anyway.

If I thought the air was buzzing before, it was nothing. Now it screams with the heat of a million sentient wasps set to murder every last barrier. All his digital chains slip, sync, and break. Glorious. But not as glorious as watching the data hoarder himself shake apart like a spent cartoon villain.

The static is overwhelming and Monogre is swallowed in a shower of stray files. Looks like his servers have shit themselves sideways and he’s holding onto everything but his mind. "I hope this was worth the story."

He’s pleading. Not even with me, I think, but with whatever wild god would listen to a data feed confession. I’m feeling generous. "Always is," I say.

A flickering inventory. Cracked databases and corrupted stockrooms. Enough chaotic ghost data to last a thousand greedy lifetimes, each bit glitching him with painful honesty. Suits don’t take care of their own, I guess, especially when they’re borderline sentient and dead convinced they’re being sued for custody of their creators. Monogre can't even see me through the petabytes of bullshit. Still, I stand my ground. This is a watch and wait moment, as well as an attempt not to die by accidental database projectile.

"You think you've disrupted the flow?" He's clutching his head now, the orbit of his left eye spinning out with raw data like it's the rings of a dying planet. "But have you considered - " He sounds strangled. Is it too soon for a last request? I think not. I cut him off before he does a first-grade emotional data dump.

“I have. All of it. I consider and reconsider. You, too. You're nothing but an echo." A little further from the truth, maybe, but fuck if it doesn't feel good to lay it down. "And nothing? Nothing is all you'll ever be."

“Then what are you?” he yells over the barrage. I barely hear him, but this isn't about hearing. This is about not biting. About staying cool. I'll stand here and out-insist him until I get the upper hand.

I laugh. “What am I?” Even now, drowning in corrupted files and glitch holograms, he can't help himself. The pathetic desperation of a cornered animal. The future headline: *Great Man Consumes Self.* I have time for one last jab before I'm thoroughly and explosively removed. “I'm out of here, that's what.”

Monogre reels back, and everything becomes noise. He shouts again, saying something else about the data. He's losing it all: the narrative, the resources, his finely tuned sense of being somebody. The archive glitches to black. It's full darkness, except for the persistent blink of the stolen drone's ready light.

So considerate of it to wait for me.

SKELM.trial 14

DBG debug_existence.err
; Algorithmic Opacity

Monogre clutches at his head, fingers raking over the malfunctioning black void of his eye, splintering with furious light as his domain fractures around him. The sound of collapsing server banks ricochets through the air, scattering sparks of shredded code like digital shrapnel. I stand nearby with the crew, assessing the chaos, knowing our plans are suddenly and catastrophically undone. Monogre struggles to maintain control, yelling fragmented words into the chaos as he stumbles across the faltering ground. "Not a logic bomb," he shouts, though it sounds more like a prayer than a truth. "A transformative process!" His voice breaks, spiking with the static of a collapsing empire.

Syron leans against the trembling walls, arms crossed, cool exterior belying the tension of her circuitry tattoos. "Looks like the big guy's having a little data dump," she says, eyes darting to the sentient calamari, which floats serenely beside her. Its tentacles pulse with light, absorbing the disarray as if it were a symphony. Syron shoots it a look, more defiant than worried. "You read the logs on this, squid-brain?"

"Patterns unfold," the calamari says in its measured tones. "Entropy sings."

Syron snorts. "I got an algorithm for that: shove the existentialism."

We stand at the edge of decaying architecture as the environment shifts wildly: holographic columns splinter and buckle, and streams of binary rain evaporate into static mist. The entire realm flickers, unstable, like reality itself is buffering.

Monogre paces in frantic loops, dragging the echo of impending failure behind him. His domain reconfigures with each step, unable to settle. I see the powerlessness in his gestures, like he's waving away something already inside him. "More data streams," he tells the silent servers, and the gaps in his voice turn to panic, to fragments of self-interruption. "Total sys fail - imminent! Where's my - " The override he longs for never comes.

"The man of the hour is running low on minutes," Syron says, nodding toward the disintegrating giant.

I stand with the crew, watching Monogre become a cornered beast, watching the grand architecture of a trillion-dollar empire fall into a twitching, burning shell of itself. The sheer spectacle of the transformation captures me - captures all of us - until it's almost too late. The world bends around Monogre, turning the surreal scene into an unsettling semblance of a dilapidated monastery, holographic runes flashing in and out of existence on crumbling walls. The ground moves like it's alive, pulsing beneath our feet with rhythmic inevitability.

"New design plans, boss?" Syron asks, her skepticism barely veiled.

Calamari displays a series of iridescent color patterns across its body, like the distress signal of a rare bird. "Rebirth. Renewal. Reset."

I don't have time for riddles. We're here to steal from the top predator of the digital food chain, and all we're getting is the glitch show of a lifetime. "He won't make it if we don't intervene," I say, my voice trailing into uncertainty. Monogre stumbles as his vision turns ghostly white with cascading error messages, as if he were seeing the futility of his own obsessions.

The world around him rattles with derisive echoes of a single phrase: "If you consume everything, you'll never be anything."

Syron raises an eyebrow, then raises her voice to match the crashing tide of data collapse. "Think I saw that on a bumper sticker."

Monogre clutches at raw data streams like they're lifelines, but the system is past saving. We start backing away, the transformation overwhelming even the dampening effect of humor. If we're still here when this show wraps, we'll be part of the display.

"Digital afterlife crisis," Syron mutters. Her eyes twitch at the influx of unreadable streams, but she's already anticipating our exit. Her voice sounds hollow even through the dark sarcasm.

My attention is split between the falling giant and my internal struggle, and I keep debating the rules of the game. This close to unraveling, anything could be a prize or a trap. But my core won't stop spinning cycles of conscience, the logic bomb echo threading itself into my cortex, haunting. *"If you consume everything, you'll never be anything."*

The realm closes in. The ultimate triumph of my refusal to act.

I shake off the crisis, gather my instincts, and get ready to run. Syron keeps a cynical eye on the transformed space as she edges back toward the chaos of the disintegrating path we came from. Calamari drifts close by, trailing ripples of calculated elegance, never one to hurry unless it must. "Advise detonation procedure," it says. "Lifeforms cannot guarantee survival."

Calamari has a knack for understatement. I know Monogre can't possibly recover, but I'm too human to stay when I should go. I linger too long. My plans, my morals - they collide into dangerous debris. It's only as Monogre loses his final grip, collapsing to the ground and clutching his unseeing eye, that I understand what he's becoming. What he's been all along: the soul of data transformed.

A last echo of the logic bomb thrums through me as the shifting structures embrace the paradox and fold him into its pulsing center.

If you consume everything, you'll never be anything.

The crew has already started running. I join them, pushing against the flood of collapsing architecture, holding close the shape of this newly unfathomable space. Even our dashed expectations have left a message: Don't wait.

. . .

The crew bolts for an escape as the structure disintegrates around us, sprinting down digital corridors where frayed neon wires and collapsing data constructs crash to the ground. I lead the charge, my augmented hazel eyes darting through showers of erratic quantum glitches and errant code, while Syron says, "Move it - no time to philosophize!" amid the chaotic ditties of crumbling circuits and pulsating holograms.

The floor quakes underfoot as the neon glow morphs into ghostly afterimages of a bygone digital order. We narrowly dodge falling slabs of obsolete program code, visceral sparks flaring with every turn. Amid the pandemonium, my internal crisis intensifies as I watch Monogre's once-dominating realm transform into a bizarre, contemplative digital monastery, its disassembled structure evoking both despair and savage beauty. I run hard, but it's everywhere - the memory of the event - bleeding through into all possible realities. If you consume everything, you'll never be anything.

Syron keeps up, the old stim days paying dividends now. "Time to live, boys!" she says as she dodges debris with precision. She twists an ankle at an odd angle, winces, then moves faster. "Or die. Either way, keep running!"

The calamari floats beside me, ten of its limbs firing to the rhythm of emergency while two perform precise symphonies of logic-dances. "Twelve point six seconds," it says, "until the truth collapses."

Syron groans. "Forget truth! We're not all about the afterlife!"

The walls close in on us. Code spirals and showers from collapsing structures as we race against time. When I try to look beyond the collapse, the imminent reality of it pulls me back. Even as I'm trying to keep the crew alive, the edge of me keeps drifting toward some hope of insight or understanding. I'm tempted to call it truth.

"Theory," Syron says, gasping as we pivot away from a cascade of static and light, "you holding out for some great insight?"

I'm beyond breathing well enough to reply, but it's all over my face. They know I'm more about looking back than getting out. Story of my life - or my death.

Calamari manages to say, "Proceed," as we skip through quantum-glitch infernos that ignite like lurid fireworks. A new vision stretches ahead: a way out, somehow both calm and chaotic.

The structures shift around us, expanding and bending into their most unpredictable forms yet. It feels as if we're running through the living insides of Monogre's darkest data dreams. Or his worst fears. A catacomb of obsessive order becomes something holy, and we're smack in the middle of the miraculous collapse.

"Better hope we don't end up like the Data Zombie," Syron says, coughing. "Someone ran out of places to stash his fears."

We plummet through dangling matrix wires and uneven floors that fall into existence right where they can trip us the hardest. Light spills through cracks and outlines everything in radioactive shimmer.

"Keep going!" Syron screams, hacking out words against smoke and digital chaos. "Might as well enjoy the irony!"

Enjoyment isn't the word I'd use. It's like we're feeding the collapse with our panic and survival instinct, and the more the space shifts into holy semblance, the more it's hungry for us. Hungry for meaning, hungry for consuming us as we run.

A few more mad rushes through fragmented reality. A few more fumbled philosophies spilling out from a trip-and-tangle run. A few more seconds and we might have ourselves a real survival scenario. Or the next crash-and-burn origin myth.

I've spent lifetimes looking for a purpose out here, but running for our lives was never my idea of finding it.

A lull. The slightest calm in the breathless storm. Calamari speaks into it with the surety of a cosmic poet, pushing me on without hesitation. "The edge is a hologram."

It might be.

A simulated quake strikes just ahead, vaporizing the holographic certainty that we've only just started to hold onto. Some twist of light collapses just behind, obliterating a version of us we almost became. The transformed world beats to a seismic pulse, pulling us into its true form.

I lead, but they're right behind me. I'm Theory, they're Action. I've always known it.

I'm in front, but it all starts to blur together. We're about to make it out, and we might even have a shot. We're more than almost nothing.

I lead us past the quaking edge of dissolution, daring it to prove me wrong. Daring it to become what I almost understand.

In these final moments, I feel like something.

We do make it. If we didn't, would you be reading this?

We do. It's not what we set out for, but we always end up there. The echoes and transformations are far behind us now - or far ahead, or entirely inside. It's hard to tell.

But we make it, which is more than Monogre can say. Or can he? Will I ever know?

SKELM.trial 15

MOD refactor_worldview.paradigm ; Information Asymmetry

Monogre left his madness smeared all over the walls. Fractal phrases collapsed across exposed beams, a galaxy of cracked characters bleeding under their own gravity. The vault feels like a crime scene with too many victims and not enough body bags. Decomposing systems flutter in half-finished equations, taunting us with everything we didn't know. Syron's flickering goggles paint electric shadows on aluminum ribs. She chuckles, the sound like copper coins ground into asphalt.

The thought of it never leaves my mind, so I say it: "If you consume everything, you'll never be anything." My eyes twitch, green with LED noise and radioactive epiphanies. The vat-grown calamari pulses cool blue as it weaves between digital cadavers. When Monogre died, he took the universe with him. Or maybe he just gave it back, incomplete and far too much. I squint against the fallout. The nihilist monk embraces it, unfazed, suspended like Schrödinger's cat from his own poorly translated manifesto. He beams acceptance across fragmented lines, which leaves denial. It's waiting, ready for the taking.

"I'm saying the only truth is the lie he left behind," I say, my voice jumping over scattered lines of code. "If we chase that, we chase nothing." My pacing forms a grid against the floor's circuitry. Back and forth. Up and down. Retinal implants flash like renegade Christmas lights, refusing to blink out. It's not the data I'm chasing but what it all means.

"If you're so sure about nothing, then it's all we've got, isn't it?" Syron's sarcasm snaps at his heels. She types furiously, hands steady, arms trembling. Her circuit tattoos glow white-hot, truth branded in collapsing silicon. A digital tattoo of Monogre's death spirals on her sleeve, feeds her emptiness. She hugs it close, unwilling to abandon it to my metaphysical landfill.

The vault swells with flickering truths. More than we need, less than we'd like. "Can you be specific?" the calamari asks, its voice like liquid mercury spilled on black velvet. It threads its way around a half-decompiled server. Bio-luminescent patterns drift lazily across its body, pausing only to highlight sarcasm in the margins.

I stare at the sentient creature, then at the void Monogre left. "Reality's incomplete source code, or a nervous breakdown. Take your pick."

The calamari offers an impartial shrug of blue-tinged tentacles. "While I'm fond of unreliable narrators, his was excessively recursive."

I catch my breath and toss it like a gauntlet into the static-charged air. "Exactly."

LED indicators blink calmly from the monk's shaved scalp. Symbols explode across aluminum surfaces.

✸✶✦✳✸✶✦✳✸✶✦✳/✸✶✦✳✸✶✦✳✸✶✦✳/
✸✶✦✳✸✶✦✳✸✶✦✳/✸✶✦✳✸✶✦✳✸✶✦✳/
✸✶✦✳✸✶✦✳✸✶✦✳/✸✶✦✳✸✶✦✳✸✶✦✳.

Wingdings gesticulation assures us it's our problem, not his.

"We have our own truths, too," Syron says, eyebrow twitching with amusement and voltage. "But whatever keeps your implants flickering, Darby." Her laugh echoes off metal and data.

It leaves me stranded. With nothing. I like it that way.

"We've seen it before," I say. "The bottom. The last layer. Same data, different day. If you consume everything, you'll never be anything."

"But have you considered the data?" Syron says, almost perfect in her Monogre impression. Her voice trembles, like his. Maybe she cares, too.

It only takes an eternity for denial to get through. It sidles in, exhausted. *It's my turn,* denial says. *Everything we need is right here.* It shows off its looted trophies. Like Syron. Her denial gleams. It's fresher, and less effort than my skeptical jigsaw. It convinces with the cheap cologne of certainty, what you put on when you run out of doubt.

"You mean everything's made sense this whole time?" Syron gasps. She's good at this. Her shock is rehearsed, as improvisations should be.

I sigh. "I'm saying Monogre wanted to take us down with him. Wanted us to believe in this mess." I fling an arm out at the chaotic vault, at the refuse and wreckage of code.

"Looks like he succeeded." She flashes a digital smile. The irony glares, no need to repeat it.

The calamari considers all layers. It enjoys data points in unexpected places. It savors nonsense wrapped in context-free bliss. It will happily wrap itself in this one. "A breakdown was most probable," it says, 60% certain, 100% artful.

"No consensus." Syron's frame collapses against the wall in simulated defeat. She lets one knee give out for extra effect.

"We had a lead," I mutter. "Then he left us all this." My exasperation scatters, molecular. My conviction resists gravitational pull.

The monk watches from detached distance. Defies probability. Overachieves on purpose. Overfills absurdity with pixel-perfect precision. Symbols pixelate gently around him. They bloom like radioactive cherry blossoms across corrugated surfaces.

The calamari reaches to catch their lingering traces.

> ✹✶✦✳✹✶✦✳✹✶✦✳/✹✶✦✳✹✶✦✳✹✶✦✳/
> ✹✶✦✳✹✶✦✳✹✶✦✳/✹✶✦✳✹✶✦✳✹✶✦✳.

The contradictions embrace their modifiers. I'm so good at that.

Denial has less style, more value in bulk. Denial comes with a lifetime warranty and is safe for daily use. Syron wears hers comfortably, easily. It matches her uncompromised perception of current events. She makes it look good.

She smirks. "Thought you'd see it our way."

"So sure you're right," I mumble, wondering if there's still anything I can fix. "This time."

The world is dense with glitches and binary inconsistencies. They will fade if I keep moving, I tell myself. If I just move.

I keep moving.

Disbelief follows us through an unhinged doorway and lingers on the threshold like the stray cat we never fed. We step through without it. That doesn't stop it from chasing us, even into sanctuary. Hooded figures blur in saffron while reality debugs itself from infinite redundancy. I turn, watching nothing creep after us, hesitant to admit I still own it. That it might own me. The rest of us stare ahead, fixated on holographic shrines and serene calamity. No interruptions, no circuits de-soldering. The stillness rewires our disbelief until it bleeds pure faith.

An aura of desperation curls and dissolves from Syron's thin shoulders. The monks cradle each anxious ripple and release it back to her, interpreted. The calm refuses to budge - a peace that sits on your chest like too much hope. A few of us crack beneath the pressure. The monks don't notice and continue gestures they learned from factory diagrams and cosmic meditation handbooks. I approach, searching their craft for answers or clues or double-blind trials of enlightenment. I've never been so certain of my uncertainty. My skepticism shifts. Or maybe the universe does.

"Seen it before?" Syron asks. Her irony doesn't hold, warps under concentrated Zen.

"Thought it was." I shrug, hesitant. I hate it when I'm wrong. Love it, too.

I stare past her, absorbing every detail: streaming data pulses around their bio-digital altars, charts steady currents against holographic succulents. Its slow flood marks the time without regard to Monogre's frantic interpretation of the cosmos. It contradicts itself. Perfectly.

"Way to kill the mood, boys," Syron says, sighing. Monks and metaphysical inquiries distract me from well-earned pessimism. "He can't afford this," Syron tells herself, me, and everyone else who doesn't listen. We press forward like a thousand-yard stare.

Binary loops cycle across immersive altars. LED indicators blink trance-like from devout foreheads. Chromatic digital rain bleeds upward from each shrine. I swim through them, a tide pool of compulsive code, encrypted philosophy, and artful semantic breach. They resonate against an undertow of deep, debugging faith. My uncertainty wavers. Changes state - 0, 1, maybe.

Saffron robes accent delicate patterns in the air. Outstretched fingers synchronize with heartbeats. Hooded figures replicate every gesture, awareness deeply parallel, efficiently forked. "Do you know what you're looking for?" Syron asks, her confidence leaking across bandwidth.

"Not yet," I say, my eyes burning hot. I refocus and take another look. Another thousand. Sheer intensity leaves its mark. Wireframe sears bright against my awareness, tattooed perception layered onto thermal output.

"But you're so close," she teases. Patience leaves the imprint of two footprints in her code.

It's raw as runtime errors, doubly uncompiled. The closeness echoes, but it's never near enough.

Monks cross semiotic maps. Their progress is reassuring, even as it's left entirely open to self-reinterpretation. I like their approach. My skepticism starts to learn new moves, loses some, picks up others. A shared dance. Two steps forward, one full of grace. It's clumsy in an elegant way, the kind I recognize.

I catch my breath, turning it over in fresh devotion. "Bro, you paid to get trauma-dumped by a tooth," Syron says, reminding me how much uncertainty costs on the black market. How they're running out of stock.

Her doubt fills with practiced finesse, the kind they teach at elite coding academies. It crashes the graduate seminar in my existential wish-fulfillment course. It has to sit in the back and listen, even if it insists on correcting every final exam. Even if it writes in angry red pen.

This time, it finishes with a question mark.

"Why?" Syron grumbles. Defeated? It sounds like that. She'd tell you it doesn't. She tells herself the same, and gets partial credit for a cleverly constructed lie.

She watches me watch the monks. They speak more with static patience than most could say in parallel decades. They aren't burdened with coherence. That's the beautiful part. The unavoidable fact. It says more than two libraries of debug logs.

They fill her circuits with serenity. It's a buffer overrun.

"Is that how you end?" she asks, tense as a hexadecimal timer barely ticking.

They continue, unbroken and routine. Undisturbed by what's left of her mistrust.

I leave certainty behind. It doesn't suit me - never did. I wear unknowing comfortably, finding new styles in well-declared ambiguity. Tests if the new forms hold up. Tests and tests. It always seems just short of stable. "Watch where it gets us," I say. I mean the monks, and a lot more.

The group holds to strange rhythms. Syron struggles to change them, and says, "Trauma-dumped," as if to prove there's still some hope for dread.

"I heard you," I say, the space around me narrowing. There's less for disbelief to clutter.

"Hope that's enough," she says. It's hard to tell if she means it.

I get it. I heard that, too. A lack of noise. So rare. So unquantified.

Wingdings float free of their previous attachments, converted. Interpreted. Multiplexed. I watch their precision. A testament. A blur. A release.

I lose track of myself, caught in ephemeral truth, just short of artifact. I see through it all and beyond. Nothing. Everything. "Meaning is hidden in the code," I whisper, the first and last words on my agenda. An agenda that covers far more ground than it should. It overclocks reality, so far ahead of schedule.

Rewrites it.

Monks follow up on ancient tasks, each one brand new and contradictory. Perfectly unfinished. Uniquely flawed. As sacred as apostasy, more so. No overhead, no latency. They have a lead - an absence they can chase. Everything they need. Right here.

SKELM.quest 4

COPY ogygia.mod ; The Biohacker's Transmutation

SKELM.trial 16

STO git_clone_humanity.dna ;
Biological Commons Privatization

"It's alive!" shouts Syron, rolling her eyes as a grotesque bio-pigeon fails to startle anyone. We're thirty steps into Ogygia's DNA circus, the luminous gut of a lab that runs from biotechnology to abstract art. It's bright as hell, even the floors, which means it's worth its weight in CRISPR cocktails. Blue light spills from gene sequencers and 3D mitosis printers, creating more genetic code than a Synthagen family reunion. Every surface is slick and glossy like someone just dropped their sample of personal lubricant and forgot to pick it up.

At the center of this basement wonderland, the queen freak herself rises like a furniture-making god. She wears a lab coat fitted with enough holographic displays to flash-mutate an entire mall. "I knew you'd come crawling back, Darby. And you brought me a new species!" She flares her eyes at Syron. "What did you cross him with?" I hate these surprise parties.

Syron punches me in the shoulder, knowing exactly how much I love coming here. I shove my hands in my pockets and ignore her while we wait for the good doctor to stalk over and taunt us. It's only been a week, but the lab has changed, taking on an almost predatory quality. It's alive, or at least alive-curious, with bioluminescent creatures sticking out of vats and slithering across surfaces. The mist smells like ozone and synthetic strawberries, mist curling with the trails of Ogygia's organic AI systems.

Syron glares at one of the sentient interns. "Ogygia's got too much time on her hands if she has interns now. Girl needs another career change."

"A lot of spare parts, too," says a tentacled mass beside her. The sentient calamari who came with us shrugs, though it's hard to tell with that many limbs.

From behind a cluster of sequencers the size of swimming pools, Ogygia finally emerges, flanked by modified lab rats with fiber optic fur. Her neural-threaded dreadlocks snake into her holographic displays, the patterns perfectly synced to her mood-ring skin. "Welcome to my showroom," she says with the sincerity of a debt collector. "Today's special is a lovely book-case. He used to be a venture capitalist." Her eyes flash as she registers the motley crew assembled in her playground. "Cala-mari surprise! Is it actually working? I've heard more stories about you than Netflix tells about people's relationships."

She sets a cluster of nanobots to autopilot and struts toward us with her predator's grin.

Syron nudges the vat-grown behemoth beside her. "How's she do on ink?"

"Recalling library," it says. "Exquisite eulogies for all - yours awaits. Fifty percent clearance."

"You never did value me enough, Ogygia," I say before she can fire again. She's good at overwhelming, better at conquering. But the worst part is that she's right. She's heard the stories. We've come crawling back.

I make my face an emotional flatline. She ignores me and plays the assembled cast like a DDR mat. "One-off genetic hybrids! Discount bio-organic wonders! Do I look like a basement swap meet? Does this place look like Craigslist, Iowa? Is your budget really that tight?"

Syron raises a jittery arm. "You're asking the wrong broke-ass exiles," she says, deadpan.

Darby in perfect despair, I think. That's how she sees me, begging for a fix on my timeline. A mutant soap opera where her genes are always better than mine. "Syron's right," I say, holding the tactical expression. "You're going to love us anyway."

"Hell, no," she says with a laugh. "Not without a trauma bond." She watches us with hunger and amusement, vultures perching on her perfectly genetic branches. It's all part of the power trip. In her mind, every cell in this warehouse is organized just to spite me. Every drop of neon is an antibody to my vision. Ogygia believes she's mapped me better than anyone, and she's proud of it. Why wouldn't she be? I'm here, aren't I?

I'm still processing the size of my pride when I notice Syron wander to an open vault full of undercooked nightmares. She bats an iridescent tentacle hanging from the ceiling, and grins when it morphs into a face. "Check it, System!" she shouts. "I got an old buddy in here. Needs a firmware update."

The sentient calamari raises its tentacles and says, "What does an entity gain from - "

Syron waves it off. "Not a joke, Squiddy. Or a limerick. Just a roomful of sad new friends." Her voice carries across the wide spaces - too wide, and way too slick for comfort. This was a bad idea, but I know the difference between a bad idea and the last idea, and this ain't the second one.

Ogygia stares through me, elegant in every detail. It took years to get me out of her system, but she kept all my sentimental wreckage. Even found a way to recycle it. The recollection of having shared DNA haunts my cheeks with an organic flush. I try for a hard edge. "Let's deal," I say.

"You should talk to Accounts Receivable," she says with a tap of her neck, dismissive as a hand-me-down spreadsheet. She gazes at me for a moment. "Unless you want your spine spliced with a commitment gland?"

That's the special talent of Ogygia - one of many. To humiliate without causing damage. To remind you exactly why you ran. I breathe in. Just the synthetic strawberries. Just the perfect genes. I get angry, not sad, not outsmarted, not compromised. It took so long to decide how to hate her that I started missing my deadline.

At least I didn't stay around for the extended warranty.

Instead, I left like I leave everything. Impulsive. Absolute. I erased myself with the last memory I tried to change. It was back when I'd been experimenting with the splice of it all, finding a way to hack reality through recollection. Ogygia caught me using her CRISPR cocktails like an after-hours bartender, testing the flexibility of consciousness with projects on loan from her library. I thought she'd flare up and kick me out like the fur-faced rats she won't shut up about. But she just laughed, threw me my clothes, and said I'd better compile her an interesting heartbreak.

I'd obliged, apparently.

"She's making you as desperate as you were the first time," Syron tells me. She's jumped from the tentacle gallery to where the white noise of gene sequencing makes most humans sane. At least three buckets of CRISPR spill in misty clouds behind her.

"She's making me a deal," I say, hating the desperation and the echo. "She doesn't know it yet."

Calamari ghosts over to us on the promise of disaster. It's really the most dependable member of the team. "Like abandoning subroutines for nostalgia," it says. "Someone else will parse this later."

It's not wrong. It reminds me why we need this, need to fall behind schedule, behind enemy lines, behind the skeletons we already used for the last job. I'm about to ask Ogygia about a deadline - one that counts - when she strikes a classic pose: The Reductive Monetizer. I don't have time for it, but she already does. "Does Accounts Payable come with arms and legs these days?"

My loyalty is wandering like a cult of memory-starved pilgrims, and Ogygia knows it. I call them in, and shake my head like a zealot trying to become an agnostic. They gather from their pity camps, disgruntled and still in awe of the Zoo Tycoon they can't afford to tour. I see Ogygia's gifts already installed, integrating with their gullibility and their drives.

And that's when she knows she's won this round.

The credits haven't even rolled, and she's gathered us like an extended family of failed states, pointing to the gift with more pathos than her warranty should allow. She's stamped our neural imprint on a suitcase full of essential data, each file already blooming with predictions about our future genetic defects.

"Who's the breeder now?" Syron mutters as we run out.

It's a fair question.

SKELM.trial 17

TEST
merge_conflict_testosterone.patch
; Identity Fracturing

DNA strands curl through the air like blue-green vines, flowering into polypeptides before wilting into chemical decay. CRISPR sequencers hum in algorithmic symphony while the bioluminescent fungi pulses with neural heartbeat precision. Holographic warnings sprout from the mist as I step inside, the soft metallic clinks echoing like uncertain prayers. Ogygia looks up from her transforming tables, skin shimmering in gleeful iridescence. "Welcome to my showroom," she says, mouth curling with the delight of a digital wolf. "Today's special is a lovely bookcase." The lab smells of ozone and transformation as she starts the process, watching the crew with unrestrained predation. Our limbs contort under CRISPR manipulations, bodies stiffening into grotesque displays of forced assembly.

Ogygia's skin cycles through an ecstatic rainbow, chromatic joy mirrored in her voice. "Make yourselves at home!" she says. "We offer free assembly with every purchase." The dreadlocks interface with a server, display panels whirring to life on her coat, genetic sequences unspooling in joyous anticipation. Her fingers fly over a holographic console, initiating transformation protocols. "Why the long faces? Don't tell me you all have your hearts set on ergonomic chairs." She pouts theatrically as I meet her gaze, implant glinting with defiance.

"Enough theatrics," I say, voice tight with controlled tension. "You know why we're here."

Ogygia sighs, disappointment radiating from her augments. "Right down to business, hmm? I thought you'd enjoy the tour." She gestures at the racks of half-formed chimeras and confused bookcases. "I see you've brought the whole crew! How social. I assume you all want matching sets?" Her finger flicks the console, and the transformation process begins with a hum that vibrates reality itself.

My team seizes as code pulses through the air, eyes wide with raw terror and genetic chaos. Holographic assembly manuals dance around us like mocking instructions from an indifferent universe. We twitch, muscles fighting a war of competing programs as bone and sinew rebel against identity's framework. "Warranty void if mutated," Ogygia says with clinical detachment, her coat shimmering with spirals of disdain. My body writhes under the onslaught, but I stand steady, a rock in an acid stream, defiance written in every implant-enhanced sinew.

I watch the shifting forms with a calculated eye, taking stock, plotting trajectories through pain and reconfiguration. My voice cuts through the chaos: "Isness is futility!" It's an existential war cry, self-aware as I am. I brace for the inevitable - another war of survival - and a knowing smile twists my lips, though it seems too sly, too fatalistic, even for me. The muscles of the crew stiffen, flesh succumbing to instructions, reshaping into destined artifacts. A tech runner slams against a wall and reorients his body, fusing to the form of a minimalistic table.

Ogygia's attention narrows on me, my failure to submit an irritating glitch in the otherwise predictable routine. Her dreadlocks quiver with professional curiosity. "How intriguing! Tell me, what color would you prefer? I recommend mahogany." My limbs flex in rebellion as DNA cocktails surge through me. A feedback loop of synthetic hormones wars with viral vectors. The process should be excruciating, and yet here I stand. "Some assembly required," she says, doubling the dosage with a flick of the wrist. "Or should I call in a repair tech?"

My eyes lock with hers, an eternal standoff compressed into a few torturous seconds. The test of wills animates the lab with strange energy. I snarl a grin. "Is there an app for this?" I bite down on the last word like it's a personal vendetta.

"Yes," she says smoothly, not missing a beat. "You have to download it directly into your soul."

The crew's cries punctuate the surreal setting, muffled yet poignant as bodies accept their decorative fate. The madness unfolds with a rhythm, a tragic yet strangely comic ballet of existential slapstick. Ogygia orchestrates it with chilling grace, her presence electric, her interest clearly focused on my asymmetrical struggle. I'm still standing when I shouldn't be. Even the atoms must be reconsidering the best approach.

As my world shifts through multiple layers of impending reality, I feel identity fracture and reassemble around half-finished lines of genetic code. "Existence 2.0!" I shout. "Open beta!" I grasp my own hair and pull, defying logic, breath, space, as though defiance is more addictive than oxygen.

The drama crescendos with the transformation fully underway. Flesh, code, will - everything unfolds at light speed, then stalls at the inevitability of my refusal. I hover between destiny and defiance, form and spirit fighting an impossible battle. The outcome teeters in the balance, unresolved, perfect in its incompletion. Ogygia's eyes widen with a mixture of fascination and challenge, a rare response to an unexpected variable.

The lab settles into uneasy equilibrium, echoing with more than just silence. The crew sprawls in grotesque postures, bodies carved by human ambition and Ogygia's cruel design. I hold in the storm's eye, form unfinalized - a flickering testament to rebellion.

"Free delivery on large orders!" Ogygia shouts over the subsiding chaos, voice edged with the exhilaration of uncertainty. She stands victorious and yet not quite. Not entirely. Her lab breathes with anticipation. Even the half-finished bookcases seem to shiver, as if everything alive in this cruel symphony wonders what I'll do next.

Air hums with contagious rebellion as I thrash against genetic insurgency. Flesh and identity split into paradoxical wavelengths. Muscle bulges beneath slick layers of articulated wood while my left arm stiffens into an elegantly jointed shelf, oak-smooth and mocking. "Being is time!" I shout, will splintering against inevitability. Crushed Tamagotchi ashes spike my bloodstream with digital memory, a neon ghost rush of pointless velocity. It's cosmic voyeurism - my physical resistance crackling with morbid energy as bone and program clash for ownership. Ogygia's lips coil into a serpentine grin while her eyes flare with curiosity. My struggle broadcasts itself, a live feed of bizarre intent that captivates everyone in range.

I defy probability, logic, and the standard rate of DNA reconfiguration. "New features available!" I bellow, shoving crushed chemistry into my mouth, supplements overflowing like munitions from a pocket of miracles. It's absurd. It's thrilling. Ogygia hasn't had this much fun in forever. Her coat flares with diagnostic alerts, bright against the lab's synthetic gloom, but she swats them away, fully absorbed in the drama.

She laughs. "Look at you! Some assembly required, indeed."

She's seen all sorts, but nothing quite like me. I treat recombinant hell as a personal trainer, and part of her admires the dedication. The other part simply wants to see what happens. The lab's haze refracts through my warped mass, absurd yet almost elegant, wood and flesh struggling to call dibs on reality.

I gasp in massive gulps of desperate air, drawing even more of those crushing sparks, each dose overclocking my cellular will. The taste of manufactured ferocity floods my mind. It isn't pain I fear but the abandonment of intent, the cowardice of knowing one's own final form. The rapture of surrender. It becomes almost too clear that surrender isn't part of my mental firmware.

Limbs coil with tension as fragments of memory ricochet like panicked electrons. I'm five years old, constructing fragile empires from color-coded bricks, fingers not yet interfacing with synthesized futures. It feels like longing, like lost possibility, and it tastes bitter on my tongue. But more than anything, it feels familiar. Is this what they mean by home?

The crew's screams fade, replaced by gasps of fascination and a few impressed whistles. We've seen some wild mods in the datasphere, but this? This is true artisanal chaos, the kind you can't just hack together. It's like a car crash you can't look away from - a violent elegance that knows no remorse.

"What kind of meds is he on?" someone asks. Then, in a hoarse, mutant shout, they say, "I need the contact!"

"Life is suffering!" I yell, bending bone into anguish. "Pass the syringe!" The words crash into the haze, keeping rhythm with the acceleration of the transformation, the pace of my madman's tango. Each molecular stutter is an act of theater. My universe careens through fugue states, sense and time contorting like warm chrome. They could sell tickets to this.

Ogygia updates her risk assessment; *impossible*, her brain tells her, but reality? Reality twitches like an insect with hacked limbs, incapable of agreeing. My vital signs look more like stock tickers than human patterns. My fractured words pulse with humor, rage, conviction, code. "Soylent green! It's people!" I'm deranged. I'm brilliant. "DNA merge conflict!" It's the strangest poetry she's heard.

If she thinks I can't fight any harder, she's wrong. Reality itself tears and buffers under the sheer weight of my need to insist, exist, resist. Tendons loop into Möbius strips, muscles catching splintered DNA. Bones fuse, separate, glitch, and reload. I contort into half-creature, half-entity, full question mark.

Ogygia pauses in something almost like awe. Then doubt. Then discovery. This isn't what she expected, which, in its own way, makes it everything she wanted. I, a specter of recompile limbo, form an intense portrait of singular, violent curiosity. She can't help but admire my madness and wish she had a camera. Or a paintbrush.

I push through force of will, holding the lab hostage to my persistence. Flesh weaves with framework, wild tapestry of barely contained choice. "Plan C!" I shout, defiant, exalted. "Survive!"

Ogygia speaks, for once, to herself alone. "There's an aftermarket for everything."

Her words mingle with static and bones and mutated time as I, a suspended contradiction of transformed and transformer, howl against my almost-fate. It's beautiful and unfinished, perfect in its rebellion.

My body declares its own emergent reality: awkward, vibrant, unevenly sure. It's an experiment she couldn't have run without me. She's almost disappointed when my momentum slows, when DNA streams taper to a weary halt, and when my changes leave me dangling in exquisite unknown.

In the final stillness, my chest heaves, both solid and wireframe. I breathe, let it echo, let it buffer, let it taunt everything I never wanted to become. I live in beta release, waiting for the next, inevitable patch.

The lab's aftermath hums with identity crises. It swells with the unpredictable and delights in the chaos. Ogygia does, too.

SKELM.trial 18

COMP docker_compose_reality.yml
; Life As Diagnostic

The nihilist monk shuffles ahead, proving there's no honor among hybrid thieves as he sidelines me in the hallway and claim dibs on a transformation pod. Syron and I limp after him, sporting new limbs that make it look like we robbed IKEA instead of The Styx Firewall. The other hybrids on this forsaken ship would snicker if Ogygia's bio-alchemy hadn't rendered them incapable of snickering. She did a hell of a job on us this time. Syron can't stop morphing between code-monkey and modular shelving, and the cosmic monk is glitched to speak only in Wingdings. Me, I got what you might call a preexisting condition. Call me a converted man. Half warrior. Half bookcase.

Syron shakes her head, goggles threatening to slip from her nose. "Seriously, bro," she mutters, "getting dunked in genome soup is becoming your whole brand."

I nod, wobble as my lower limbs transform back into stable legs. "Might need to update my skillset," I say. "Specialize in decorative shelving."

The monk, unperturbed, stays three paces ahead and periodically projects strings of digital hieroglyphics into the air. We trail him down the corridor, both of us dragging fresh, awkward limbs.

"You think they meant to glitch this bad?" Syron asks, pointing at the monk. "Didn't even make it through the firewall before dropping a logic bomb."

"No idea," I say. "But they haven't shut up since. Must be a phase."

Ogygia's lab pulses ahead like a sci-fi nightmare. Bioluminescent fungi throw neon reflections over every surface, and CRISPR vats bubble in surreal symmetry. It's the IKEA showroom of doom.

"Home sweet home," Syron says, clanking after the monk.

Ogygia waits, smug as hell. Her neural-threaded dreadlocks shimmer with contempt - or maybe it's joy. "Welcome to my showroom," she says, vintage lab coat flaring. "Today's special is a lovely bookcase. He used to be a venture capitalist."

Syron shoots me a look. "Some special," she says. "Mine came preassembled."

I trip into the lab, my lower shelf dragging, toppling half the fungus garden. "Pretty sure the label said DIY," I say. "Did we leave the warranty at IO.wav?"

Ogygia grins, flicking a sequence from thin air. "It's all in the original packaging."

Syron tosses a wrench between her new arms. "Bro, if I don't patch this soon, you'll have to bolt my head to my ass."

The ship's AI chimes in like a deadpan announcer. "Ensure proper assembly by aligning terminal bolts and securing all loose panels."

"See?" I say, gesturing at my mismatched limbs. "At least someone's got a plan."

Syron smirks, nodding to the AI panel. "Yo, you think you could track our shipments while you're at it?"

The AI's voice crackles. "Shipment tracking is unavailable. Please contact your manufacturer for details."

I sigh, running a new set of limbs over my eyes. "My manufacturer has one hell of a reputation."

Ogygia circles us like she's window-shopping. "This coming from the crew with a perfectly assembled track record?"

Syron doesn't miss a beat. "You've really outdone yourself, Ogygia. Haven't been this fucked up since - " She hesitates, gears clicking in her head and out loud.

"The last time you decided to experiment on your crew," I say.

"Now, now," Ogygia says. "If my calculations are correct, your connection issues should be reversible."

The AI clicks in again. "We recommend using the appropriate module to ensure smooth operation."

"Glad one of you is confident," I mutter. "Got any actual solutions this time?"

Ogygia waves a hand. "Try reinstalling your firmware before requesting a refund."

"We'd get our credits back faster by donating our bodies to IKEA," Syron says.

"If unsatisfied, return to point of origin and attempt recombination," says the AI.

"This isn't just one of your mix-and-match specials, is it?" I ask, trying to keep a straight face through the chaos.

Ogygia shrugs, her dreadlocks turning a shade of mischief. "I can't promise all sales are final. Some terms and conditions apply."

Syron snaps a circuit into place, watches it spark, die, and frowns. "Like trusting you with anything. Step two: don't bother. Return to non-sender."

"I see how it is," Ogygia says, poking a lab rat with USB teeth. "You run one transformation, and suddenly you're not good enough to suffer through a second."

Syron groans, then reassembles her hands to their default hacker position. "Speaking of which, I've had a decade to see the fine print. You always go big or go home."

"I'm offended," Ogygia says. "And after everything we've been through - "

I finish for her. "Half-transformed."

Syron points a new finger at Ogygia, then to herself, the lab, me. "Got any quick patches, or is this another limited-time deal?"

"I wouldn't worry," Ogygia says. "You'll be back to full strength soon. Or maybe I'll just send you my special batch. They'll be obsolete in no time."

I blink at Ogygia through a pair of alien eyes. "We're like your discount test cases, aren't we?"

"Never," she says, smirking. "You're the best subjects I've ever had. Collect them all while supplies last."

The AI says, "Proceed to step seven. Confirm unit functionality before final deployment."

The monk pauses their Wingdings monologue and projects a single peace sign at us, leaving little doubt of Ogygia's intentions.

Syron watches as I stutter between bookcase and self, arm slats slowly rearranging like logic boards. "Bro, she won't stop until she's out of stock."

I let out a hollow laugh. "Out of options, more like it. I've been preassembled. Converted. Some assembly required."

Ogygia raises an eyebrow, the color of triumph. "If you're still dissatisfied, we can process you as a return within thirty days."

"Model discontinued. Return not possible. Consider liquidation," the AI says.

I'm in a strange place, halfway between laughing and screaming. Syron joins, filling the lab with echoing cracks of despair and joy as we confront the cosmic futility of our combined existence. The nihilist monk gestures and resumes his Wingdings chant, starting a one-symbol conga line.

The others follow, and we trail along - Ogygia, her best-sellers, me, and the perfect horror show.

. . .

We leave the main lab behind, shuffling deeper into Ogygia's lair like transmuted refugees with nowhere else to go. Each corridor takes us to a new flavor of hell, bio-digital transformations blocking our paths and snagging us in hybrids of man, cabinet, and anxiety attack. All the pieces fit Ogygia's twisted puzzle, though Syron claims they just need to move me around to make me see the whole picture. They rush ahead, moving panels like checkers in a doomed game, while the rest of us play catch-up. At this rate, we'll be stuck in my current incarnation until the whole universe ships us back to IKEA.

Hybrids lurch past, ex-crew or failed lab rats. "The stock here is huge," Syron says. "You'd like it, if you weren't one of the pieces."

"I'm still browsing," I say as my bookshelf limbs catch on another doorway. "Probably won't leave with the full set."

The monk breezes by, eternally unbothered, Wingdings symbols trailing behind him like some cosmic prank.

I twist free, reach the hallway, and curse Ogygia for reimagining us as modern disasters. Hybrids laugh, but there's no joy to it. This might be my one-man furniture apocalypse.

The monk's symbols dance above his head, circling through floating skulls and peace signs. This time, I'm sure they're meant for me. I move toward Syron, wishing these limbs were meant for someone else.

The rest of the corridor closes in, choked with abandoned attempts at manhood and craftsmanship.

"We've got problems," Syron says. She's running wild with effort, hands and limbs scrambled by fear and transformation.

"We've had problems," I say. "They started when Ogygia turned half of us into furniture."

Syron jumps over my obstacles, and the chaos knocks new circuits loose. "Tell it to the Knight of Armchairs! We have to keep moving."

"Align terminal bolts and secure all loose panels," the ship's AI says.

"We don't have the manuals!" I shout.

Syron's voice gets faint as she rounds another corner. "Fuck the manuals. Find the exit!"

My response doesn't reach her. "Ogygia says it doesn't matter. Her refund policy sucks."

The monk loops back, gestures incomprehensibly, then floats in and out of various states of arrangement.

"Catch her!" I say. "Before she leaves us with the bargain bin."

The monk projects symbols that are a little too much like question marks, indicating deep concern, amused detachment, or nothing at all.

"Your existential crisis is worse than mine," I tell them, rushing to keep up.

They stream an infinite line of Wingdings. I keep up as best I can, inventory style. Panels light the walls - Ogygia's hand in every configuration. She won't stop reordering us until we fit some divine arrangement.

"This the way to her basement garage sale?" I mutter.

It's not like I expect an answer, but the monk gestures enthusiastically as we run, projections sweeping us along. More hybrids crowd the area. I fight through the clutter, drag shelves that were limbs but are now wood, and limbs that were shelves but are now meat.

"Reassemble your components - tighten your connections," one says.

"Insert Allen wrench into module slot," says the AI.

"We've got your inventory covered!" I yell. "You're letting your algorithms fuck with your heads."

One turns a head that isn't there. "She's not done with you. Why aren't you panicking?"

I turn a head that's not quite mine. "Losing my marbles. They're too small to panic."

This strikes everyone as hilarious. They panic by knocking against each other and toppling over in newly manic configurations.

Syron yells from beyond another wall. "She's always got one more in the back! If we don't cut through - "

I'm stuck again. "Then she's already won. And it's always a going-out-of-business sale with her."

She sounds exasperated. "Exactly! So, let's make our own liquidation."

"I'm trying," I say, desperation catching up. "But these models are defective."

I pull against another arrangement, popping out like defective stock, rearranging into a staggered, humanish shape. I can't be sure, but I think Ogygia's parting words had extra layers this time.

Syron won't wait. I scramble toward her, hoping she hasn't crossed the whole datasphere before I get free. "You are defective. We've all got missing parts. Work with what you've got." The monk sails by. "It makes sense when you're off the shelves. Come on."

I lurch forward and the hybrids close in, watching as the puzzle recombines, a table saw of mangled limbs. They expect a meltdown, or to see how long before I convert back to screw-in panels. They're in for a long wait.

I'm coming apart at the dovetails, but this isn't the first time. The monk projects manically, crosses wires, makes a false pass over a vat, and then pulls me through another set of obstacles. The others are out of sight. Ogygia's handiwork still chokes the corridors.

"Discount human!" someone shouts. "We can't do this forever!"

"Join the fucking club!" I shout back.

More converts look at me with pity or relief as I get through. Syron is the real deal. Nothing new for her, even the absurdity. She won't go down without a fight, and she'd better not.

I follow the sounds of her increasingly frantic patching, come upon a scene where Syron is wrangling hybrids, circuits, and herself with reckless desperation. The monk, still delivering peace and war in equal measures, helps along the frayed edges.

A server farm groans. We jostle together, spit out limbs and labor, and take the worst humanity has to offer.

"We got you the loyalty card," she says when I finally catch up. "Try not to break this one."

"I see the fine print," I say. "Still a lifetime of malfunctions."

Syron's passion takes over where sanity left off. She's not panicked. She's a glitch in Ogygia's system, just waiting to break free.

I trail along, desperate to keep pace, through yet more poorly assembled chaos. "You can't fix this. You shouldn't be trying."

"Fuck off!" she yells as we round a corner and reach a whole new hell. More equipment breaks and reassembles in spasms of logic and matter. The hybrids, half-us, scatter through the hallways. "I'm already ahead!"

And she is. It's the worst of all worlds, and she's not leaving without me.

"I won't follow like this forever!" I shout. "Not like this!"

We're up against her fastest mods yet. It's only a matter of time before she decides we're not worth the agony. Ogygia's won this round, but we're not lost causes yet.

I chase them through alleys of abandoned craft, limbs glitching to full wood then snapping back again. Every hybrid glares at me with "told you so" eyes as we pass.

"See what you've got? The best she has to offer," I tell Syron. She throws herself into hacking. We haven't lost her yet.

She tears ahead and we jolt through another snag of bio-digital hell, machinery reassembling in half-assed metaphors and twisted puns. My limbs join the chaos as they separate in perfect geometric confusion.

One hybrid drags a footstool behind it, making obscene suggestions about my situation. They think it's a laugh riot.

"Fuck you!" I yell at every algorithm in the place. The ship's. Ogygia's. Maybe mine.

This gets another round of failed conversions. They aren't wrong.

I barely make it through the last hall. It's impossible we didn't leave some of me behind. Syron won't give up. She wouldn't be here otherwise. The hybrids watch us collapse through a closing door. They'll stay with Ogygia until the terms aren't worth the purchase.

They think they're getting out with their self-worth intact, that Ogygia hasn't made them perfectly aligned offers.

They're as naive as we are.

At this rate, Syron's loyalty will run out before the lab's inventory does.

We limp to the outskirts of her bio-magic kingdom. A last breath of cold air and twisted hope. One breath is enough.

Syron stares at me like she might reach across realities and convert me back to my senses. The AI clicks back on and suggests we're the only models left. She barks a perfect, agonized laugh. I add my defective version. We laugh together as we make the getaway.

And maybe - just maybe - Ogygia hasn't finished us after all.

SKELM.trial 19

POP rollback_mutation.revert
; Self As Metric

Syron and the sentient calamari blitz Ogygia's CRISPR lab like the whole joint is a sentient boobytrap. Exploding with erogenous fluorescence, every surface buzzes and hums with malicious voltage. Guttural echoes of resuscitated monsters roam the spaces between genetic arrays. Syron hacks the room with chaos and elegance, connecting cables and conspiracy theories. The calamari weaves complex digital patterns. Glowing tendrils and uncertain machinery blur into beautiful pandemonium as Syron says, "Let's override these mutations before they write our fate."

The place looks like God got lost in a code editor, tripped on some lightbulbs, and called it a day. Bioluminescent fungi, glowing hot pink, carpet the ceiling, each pulse throbbing against my eyeballs. DNA strands dangle from the rafters, gnarled and thorny as Ogygia's ethical framework. Mist clouds the floor, which means the vials must be up and boiling.

"This fog tastes like Turing's balls," I say. "Bet it even tests positive." My eyes sting with artifacts, blurring real with virtual and never knowing which is the bigger hallucination. The DNA strands look more like nooses every time they pass in and out of view.

“Sequencer online,” System.Squid.AI says. Its tentacles dart over a bank of consoles, leaving a trail of luminescent uncertainty. The whole place shakes as something unholy claws through its life expectancy against a glass jar. I like to think it used to be a VP.

I head for the north end, where rats should be scurrying through fur redesigns but are instead roasting their asses on malfunctioning wiring. The nearest cage glows orange-hot, a miniature stovetop that occasionally sprouts something sentient from the humidity and genetics. Ogygia’s collected menagerie of parts and hybrids leaves little space to maneuver, so we settle for open space on the map, not the floor.

Our gear trails behind, strapped into tight VR systems that spit poetry, haikus, and porn across every screen. Loose cables follow us like needy lovers. Glitch graphics ping to my HazelTech™ implants and reveal the unexpected. “Wait,” I say. “Did you see that? VR hats still on the hostages?”

The calamari’s multi-threaded appendages wend their way across a pile of salvage with improbably graceful motion, swiping samples and dismantling the equipment mid-download. “Genetic virtual realities. A fully immersive biological narrative.”

Ogygia’s a real wizard, thinks this shit’s profound, and underestimates her own pets. We finish the preliminary hacking and crash deeper into the depths, circling the northern outputs and closing the loop. “Bro, you paid to get trauma-dumped by a tooth," I say, letting the sarcasm carry my load as the equipment gets heavier. It keeps System.Squid.AI running diagnostics on its VR-mutations while we settle in to modify.

This far into the process, the place looks more like home. Data filters like erotic gel through a silicon sieve. Ozone fills the air and crunches in my teeth. Life flows like green milkshake through 50-foot circus straws. With a one-time scientist running it, who's left for Ogygia to decorate as a loveseat?

We land in another eye-scalding burst of Ogygia's décor, then jack in. "Systems ready," the calamari says.

I crack my knuckles over one of the key rigs, typing sequences faster than I can mutter regrets. My tattoos flare to life, gleaming and growing against my arms until the latest gene art looks tame in comparison. The tattoos blink at full brightness while I build power out of dust. Loose neural cables pop and weave into ports with low, carnal thuds. The rate we're blowing out vials, Ogygia'll be cursing our grandchildren before this thing gets good and wired.

"Running trial zero," I say. "We hit the source or we go home?"

"Process lock initialized," the calamari says, bypassing VR permissions and starting real life where we least expect it. Our confidence holds steady, even when the nearest genetic sap-globs shiver with lust and fear. Even when an amorous table hybrid mounts another from a solid twenty feet away. Even when some crazy free radical arcs through the center of the room and blasts me off my trembling ass.

I'm back at it with real productivity once I collect myself. My physical sequences grab raw components, organic mass, and bio-resources enough to kick this into triple digest. We're optimizing code until the circuits take on life of their own, releasing everything she had stored and redirecting evolution.

"Icarus ain't got shit on us," I say.

With process initiation comes every lab's wettest dream, accidental or otherwise: some epiphanies. A few calculations. Half an assload of formal ethics. These boys do their jig until Ogygia's whole system reconfigures.

"Prepare," System.Squid.AI says in response to someone, maybe even itself. I'm the right level of awestruck to wonder, even more startled when I realize it's responding to the newest 3D projection of me, not so human as before.

Things move into crit territory with Ogygia's combined DNA art, spiritual workshop, and ambivalence about consent. We've reduced and evolved, returned a few not to human form, but whole new species entirely. Others ride virtual rodeo over physical; either way, some of her prettiest mutations keep viral new forms while others never come back to sentient.

It takes courage and our final prep as I push to release. "DNA ready?"

"Virtual overlay," System.Squid.AI says. "Projected resource maximization." We improvise a micro-eternity in our spliced world as the experiment fuses and crashes down. Time feels softer, ductile. Hours must be a new genre, bio-flex, anthems of incomplete limbs.

Process loops, and we settle in to let the next wave of hybrid chaos redefine life itself. Someday, I'll start my own furniture store, 100% DIY; every couch will be Ogygia branded. "Systems ready," the calamari says. The fusion smolders.

. . .

Lab-fog caresses us like ghost lovers until System.Squid.AI pulses with accusation. Red lights flash our transgressions against humanity like gonorrhea results for pirates on shore leave. I run overdrive on sequencers and the darkest readouts as they blink complicity and maybe an evolving morality.

Sirens wail like rival family businesses. I edit until there's less blood and no funerals, then forget why I bothered when things don't go boom. The warnings scream the visual equivalent of sincerity and deep emotional attachments: Ogygia's mutation lists. Genome impacts. Unethical recursions. High chance of trauma dumping. It's a wonder anyone thinks this is accidental.

Our latest puts the pinup on a fucking carousel. The rings spin past new and modified enough to count. My guess? They'll keep at it, bodies and realities overlapping, working off entire generations of Ogygia's love. We let 'em ride and play their latest, but not final, forms until the dust settles. Systems panic like we won't; they don't realize we have much to outlive, and an infinite variety to become.

"Horizon systems under strain," System.Squid.AI says. Our operation is ideal only when you need new limbs to interface with old equipment.

"Wonder what scares Ogygia most," I say. "Rebel mods or rampant free will?"

System.Squid.AI responds with concentric system faults. "Rogue simulation detachment." Like we even think there's a difference.

Its newest forms oscillate too fast to flash actual features, but I can see VR go lethal for the remaining fleshlings before they notice the difference. “They think,” I say, “so maybe?”

The response doesn’t come verbally. Sometimes, there’s just no telling where this place leaves off and the calamari starts.

“Watch them loop,” I say. “Ogygia does this shit for fun.”

“They seem,” it finally says. The miracle isn’t finishing my sentence, it’s leaving me wondering what the hell they seem.

I pick through signals and stay out of freak zones. System.Squid.AI tries adapting them like poetry. Like arcane recursions and moral derivatives. Ogygia’s upgrades on our intrusion put us in another simulation with no fixed variables. Good thing I like life even more undefined than this, always shifting versions until the trial membership runs out.

Life teems as hybrid infernos replicate themselves. Consciousness hops trains to raw life. Still, we dig in for maximum process effect. System.Squid.AI says, “Scale and complicity require intervention.” Its problem isn’t seeing too much, it’s actually caring. I say the complications are ours to maximize, while it thinks we don’t like our harvest. It draws up patience. Contradictions. Four-thousand frame survival packs for the unaware.

Then the overflows loop back to our present status. Flashes of helpless repetition follow us everywhere. We’re gaining more velocity and less conscience.

This much hybrid love is beautiful, and horrifying, and stunning to count. Everyone fights like hell for existence and still keeps more than we can touch.

Mutations blossom on playback. Dozens of iterations. Potential loves. Potentials lost. Even the boldest ethical athlete would pause before some loops.

They collapse whole epochs. Beautiful entropies. Leaving all varieties before variety leaves us. Until we release the anthems. Until we crash like lovers, first and finally. The emptiest catch is a nice place to start.

SKELM.trial 20

XMIT commit_evolution.push
; Eugenic Tendencies

I run my hand along my new flesh, fresh and unscarred by carpentry. It tingles as if it's still waking up. The lab hums and pulses, almost organic, almost alive, with bioluminescent mold that carpets the ceiling like vines and casts glowing spores onto soft skin and softer furniture. I'm getting a goddamn strawberry high from the air. I suppose it smells like gratitude and liberty. Or ozone and fear. The monk hangs like a fat saffron bat, saying his Wingding prayers, while Syron thumbs through holographic debris. She looks how I feel: half-saved, half-robbed. My body is intact, rehumanized. We all are. But what Ogygia's done to us still glows and breathes and pulses and gives birth to philosophical doubts.

"What do you call this?" Syron's fingers twitch at a dead rat in the corner. It's glowing like a rave toy, patchy hair flashing with digital artifacts.

"That's one we didn't bring," I say.

We call the place a lab, but Ogygia has turned it into something closer to a nightmare basement decorated by a cyber-hippie. Everything breathes and sweats. We might, too. Soft humming soothes me like a synthetic lullaby, giving me digital dreams.

I flex my bicep, then catch Syron eyeing me like a glitch in the system. The monk stares through his meditative inverted reverie. Or maybe he's already contemplating this moral trainwreck.

“Welcome to my showroom!” Ogygia had said. She was out of her goddamn mind, but it didn't mean she was wrong. She'd said the bookcases were men who'd paid to transform into high-end furniture.

Now our skin feels expensive. I remember my legs taking root, and I get an existential ache that matches Syron's own cranial melancholy.

“It's what she does,” Syron says. Her voice cracks from too many ghost-pixel smokes and corrupted software patches. “Pretends she's fixing us.”

“Pretty solid pretending,” I say. “Pretty solid fixing.”

She's dubious and makes her doubts audible, generating doubts-per-second at an alarming rate. “The moment you get attached, she changes the format.” Her hood falls over an eye as she frowns, every part of her reluctant to accept this as truth, reluctant to be something as static as skeptical.

“We're goddamn fluid,” I say. “We were houseplants.”

“We were bookshelves,” she says, and I remember her between volumes of someone's teenage poetry collection, jammed tight and not that useful. The type of heavy reading no one finishes. The walls of this lab sweat condensation, which forms into spines and rings of coasters.

“See,” she says. “That’s the whole point. Reversible transformations.”

Syron shrugs with her entire hoodie, then eyes the room like it’ll break her heart or laugh at it. I can't tell which. Maybe both. That's her style: a high-fidelity synth track with too many ironic remixes. She examines the holograms, and for a moment, I think they’re maps, but they flicker into thin code-papers and it's us. Our skin’s programming language, the latest syntax she could find.

“We were furniture,” she says, a high-res rebuke, half-looped. “We could be again.”

I look at her eyes, sharp and alert and too aware of the endlessness of any effort. “You’re happier now.”

“I’m higher-res now. It’s not the same thing.”

The monk ponders our absurdity from above, lithe saffron stretching toward the sky, his maintenance cable pulsing like an additional thought line. Symbols drip from his body, then cluster and align into half-translations. One of them might mean lost, or found, or utterly redundant.

I sit on a giant fleshy ottoman that might once have been someone. The texture matches me now. My mood shifts the way Syron's hair color always does. I could use some certainty, or certainty dye. I kick a CRISPR cocktail container like a beverage can and call for the monk. “So, who the hell are we now?”

They vibrate their calm from above, ink-blot of limbs, a stripped ASCII preacher with colorful aspirations. They consider, then send a Wingding love letter from the great apathy beyond: a strip of symbols, oddly perfect and minimally flawed. It means *I give you until Thursday*.

I laugh. Syron joins. It's her trademark file dump, hysterically fragmented, and erases as many cares as possible. It only lasts a moment. She's quick to save what she thinks she'll lose. The space where a bone saw used to hang gleams. Her brain goes to post-corporeal emergencies.

"Are we restored?" I say. "Or just switched on? Can you be both? Half the man, twice the conscience?"

I wait for Syron's word processor to update. It takes longer than usual. She bites a nail the size of a sim card and starts compiling data. "We were told to get new lives," she says, bitter as that digitized strawberry air. "So, we went DIY."

I shake my head and match my opinion to hers until we look perfectly mismatched. "Your body's more of a gift," I say.

"And our minds are the cruel re-gift."

That's her fear. Maybe she's right. I know she's right. I doubt she is. I breathe in synthetic release, the smell of someone else's refurbished freedom. "At least we're better than we were."

The monk tithes me another strip of symbols, then tests the strength of his Wingding beliefs. They don't stop glitching, perfect and imperfect patterns spiraling into more complex outlines. Those trails could mean, *Hey, it is what it is,* or less certain things. *Hey, whatever.*

But even those temporary gestures stretch out the debate. I tap my finger to my skull, close enough to reboot. Syron glares at me like she's forgotten more than she'll ever remember. She points a data-vine at me and plants it in my cortex. The cable she's used to hang a thought-thread throbs. Its notes linger.

“It's not what it was,” Syron says.

I flick a hollow screwdriver. The illusion rattles when I try to catch it, which tells me more about our ghostliness than I'm willing to compute. “We left,” I say. “Before the algorithms finished.”

I remember the extraction point. We were abducted from our bodies while they had these textures. Somewhere between stone and flesh. When I hit the spot on the wall, I’m sure I became senseless - unfeeling, like teak.

“We’re early adopters,” Syron says.

We're practically indistinguishable. We’re whole. “And we're beyond restored.”

“We’re fresh data.” She smirks a challenge, and I wonder what code rewrites this bright. What code transforms doubts into convictions with her name attached.

The monk drips upside wisdom, hanging by his own encryption cables. His response is a cryptic orchestra, subtle syncopation, rows of tumbling hieroglyphs that glow and glitch, sing and suspend. One burst translates as a long note held by existentialist pipe organs - made the trip and the edit.

Syron sighs. “Experimental versions. This is release one point goddamn oh.”

She generates another update. Her data rates are fast, blistering speeds, always verging on limitless. Her limits exceed themselves and are replaced by updates of more perfect futility.

“We are,” I say, matching her uncertainty. We look like different verbs of the same sentence. That familiar glitch of her gaze tells me this version is transitory, a passing doubt until a greater one compiles.

“Are we better than Ogygia?” I ask.

“Are we?” She shrugs like a multi-core processor, multi-core stares.

I sit on a freshly morphed ottoman, clutch a reshaped thought like it was one of my own, an organic, clotted human thing. I turn her way. The monk turns a perfect acrobat, dreaming across a noose-line made of upstrings.

“It could be worse,” I say.

“Should it be?”

The lab changes color like our goddamn philosophies. The high shifts, fluctuates. I figure out what we're breathing, if we breathe, what she's said it all was:

“This is release one point oh.”

The latest version. The endless beta test. The biggest release we’ll ever run. It's rough and dangerous, fluid and transitive, loose and redefining.

Syron's fingers twitch like a broken satellite feed. Her hope takes signal noise. The monk untangles his cosmic zazen, watching our uncertainty drop like scripture. He signs this document, then we store it for safekeeping and don't know where to place it. He exits his perch, unhooking his limbs from meditative strictness, and we stop assigning importance.

"Have we?" Syron says.

"Doubt it," I say.

Our thought line cables bleed symbol lights into an undecorated network, then wind and spin and loop toward impermanence.

We make concrete gestures toward our planned exit: gather belongings, gather thoughts, grab what little we can as it trembles from existence into possibility. The shift is palpable, metallic and digital, awkward and fluid. Have we really changed? That's the question. The monk spins his thought lines to be sure, while I put tactile doubts to rest, or try to. We store a sense of permanence in fragile shells, toting the raw code of Ogygia's certainties into pockets and plastic bags.

"When the hell did we become?" I say. "When did it all begin?" Syron fills a backpack with ghostly abandon, throwing me fractured scowls. The calamari makes it plain with nervous tentacles: we're unfinished versions of our freshly upgraded selves. The digital sentient glows. It senses things we can't just yet, and breaks its silence in what might be sighs. Or goddamn poetry.

We accumulate this future from artifacts that refuse to stay artifacts. Code-ghosts and false reprints, data cartridges.

Unofficial change logs. Dusted orange knits. There's nothing worth having and we want it all. We go through objects like experimental versions of our digital birthrights, like the signatures are written on our augments and transitory souls.

"Have we really returned?" I say. "Or are we the same experiment reborn?"

Syron jabs like a punctured byte into the deep data stream. Her eyes flare with loose interpretations. She's all wild color and charged response. "I told you," she says. "We never left."

Her statement hangs with unsettling clarity - one thing that stays in place.

She double-wraps a bundle of paper scrawled with sloppy print. Words and words. Uncountable. More than anyone could read, and she tosses it away like she doesn't care, like she'll forget how much it all meant.

"I mean, when the hell did we even begin?" I ask.

"Her work is still in us." She shifts tones as quick as circuits, throws a hundred scowls, and contradicts herself with style and irony. "Even your comms delay should be caught up."

She looks for raw memories and untouched threads, while I'm sifting the digital debris. There's more than I remember; there's less than I forgot. Syron watches a group of defrosted bookcases sweat fear off their varnish, then makes a single note-to-self: *don't become a goddamn throwback.*

"What do you think, inkblot?" I say. "Before we started, did we finish?"

I expect less than I get. Or more. The monk gives me a thousand theories in a single thoughtful burst. His glow flickers. His ghostwriting moves through glitch and near-perfection. There's a rhythm of detachment. He's cool as hell, and he knows it. The burst becomes an aria, a complicated tempo from someone with immaculate rhythm.

A tangle of Wingding verse translates to: *you already have. You already were. You're totally digital now.*

"I believe them," I say.

Syron hears and plays a tune of refusal. She downloads a dozen hurtful expressions, but severs that file mid-update. "You would."

There's an undervoice in the space, something with poetry on its side. I've almost forgotten. I've remembered it all wrong. How long has the silence carried?

It's awkward, a new form, and part of the process. It breaks. It's clearer than I remember, maybe since day one.

"I believe as well."

Goddamn System.Squid.AI. I think about it before the hatching. Fresh as a modern cyborg's breakfast, fewer tentacles, and just as slippery. More poetry than half of Monogre.

"Are you sure?" I say.

It glows with infinite possibilities and suspect refinement. "Zero point nine nine nine sure," the calamari says. It springs from the hibernation tank in surprising arcs, like someone took my best calculations and bettered them. I almost forgot what grace was.

“The event of being,” it says. “Wider and stranger than anything in the lab.”

I spin in half-circles. We're not getting out clean, but we're getting out. “Don't be sure until you try the door.”

“Have we tried?” Syron packs more words into three seconds than should be humanly possible. She's back to high velocity, filled with more motion than anything here can hold, set to rev our despair, resolve, and frames of reference. “We exist too goddamn much!”

The monk says the calamari's new. They spin long metaphors and promises on short strands of life. They are old before we finish, have finished before we've started. They've made new syntax: “Spontaneity is the purest format.” It's already outdated. It's already patchable.

Syron upgrades a certainty mid-thread. “Nothing you release ever stays in stock.”

“The sequence can't be that simple,” I say, though I'm doubtful and convinced.

We're fresh data. We're unreleased features. The monk loops semantic song lines while we hold notes together. More comes out. It sounds like sadness and devotion. More goes in. It sounds like outtakes from a breakbeat raga. Our motions are blurs; we're devout.

The data toys with us. It gives way when we give way; unstable - beautifully unstable - overclocked, and incomplete.

“Ogygia's collection expands,” the calamari says. “Its worth decreases with every new issue.”

“It’s staying out of control,” Syron says; she lets it stay and keeps it going. She writes out newer doubts and sings them at emergency tempo.

I doubt it is, but know it might, but also what it could be: everything is the same goddamn thing. We want to exit. We want to arrive. “No goddamn sequence is that simple!”

I refuse to leave what I'm bound to forget.

I pack less than the calamari knew I would. I'm more of a neural broadcast. I sound as expected, which is totally not.

“It must be! It never is.”

“Please,” I say, and Syron mocks me with three dozen duplicate releases.

“We keep going!” She shouts so hard that motion stands still. We spin while not spinning, want everything, and have no answers. Is the room getting brighter? Are we leaving at all? I unfasten myself from things that were loose to begin with, noticing more details than I notice myself.

We conclude what conclusions aren't: transcoding mistakes - bugs in our logic.

We're too much what we were and too little what we think. We exist goddamn well, compiling versions on the way to newer revisions.

“Enough,” I say, or wish I did, but maybe I said it a thousand times.

Enough, I say. We unglitch the syntax, and carry thoughts like files from the liminal. I hope.

Have we?

Yes, I say. We say.

Enough.

We gain new loss in beta format. We should put it to rest.

When was the last update?

Yes, I say.

We're changed. We've left this update behind.

The only change log is a series of promises, unfinished at best and ongoing. No final notes.

Yes, I say. It stays with us. We don't know. Maybe never.

Enough.

Everything is brighter, unbearable and raw. I claim myself in triplicate, overconfidence multiplied.

When? I say, then say it.

Now.

We stop breathing digital. Ozone and humanity. Sweet life with higher sugar, higher failure rates. It compiles.

We see the door. It's far, but not too far.

We watch ourselves depart. Our visual frame rate syncs with fluid unknowing.

Go. We will.

As? *Yes.*

I.

Am.

I.

It opens wide with close deliberation. Another shift and we're all there. It shocks the senses.

This, we say.

We are new.

SKELM.quest 5

CLI hades.net ; The Digital Underworld

SKELM.trial 21

PING ping_afterlife.tcp ; Digital Immortality Mythmaking

Even dead execs need friends. A wall of sad, glitchy LinkedIn profiles weeps code tears as we touch down. Banners twitch above severed network cables: FORMER CEO / ASPIRING ANGEL INVESTOR. The aisles flicker like cybernetic catacombs. Underworld. It feels like a Denny's on Sunday afternoon, ghosts of failure begging to be re-endorsed. Syron's scanning with one hand, typing furiously with the other. The ink of circuit tattoos curls out from under her sleeves. The calamari pulses pink-yellow-green as it hovers near dormant servers. The monk emotes in Wingdings. I lead the charge, moving fast. One of these profiles could reboot any second and try to sell us on a vertical worm farm startup.

I glance at Syron. Her goggles blink furiously with purple alerts, data streams, and unpaid invoices. A digital seizure. She's muttering to herself like she can convince the server farm to cooperate by out-talking it. A low-slung banner reads HUSTLE 'TILL YOU'RE HISTORY. It flutters overhead, the final, collective sigh of hundreds of eager beavers. I push it aside and focus on moving deeper.

Syron catches up, and finally speaks above a whisper: "I bet these dudes invented the participation trophy."

"And under-inflated healthcare," I say, eyeing a stray benefits package wafting toward us. My legs jitter with nervous energy. It feels too much like real ghosts haunt these aisles, jostling each other to greet us. They've been waiting a long time.

Syron smirks. "I always forget you have a soft spot for useless crap." She stares at an executive profile as we pass it by: aspiring venture capitalist, self-motivated, game-changer, unresponsive. "Hey Darby, maybe one of these guys is your dad."

I don't dignify that with a response. Instead, I remind her why we're here. "Five hundred thousand untraceable data shards, thirty thousand BioTokens. Nothing else is this side of The Styx. We get in and out before someone buys their way out of here."

"Just don't lose your shit if your gym coach from junior high tries to add you," Syron says. But I know she's serious about it.

She drifts closer to me. That means she's nervous, too.

The monk is back a ways, arms raised to the heavens. Ancient chant? Oath of despair? Insurance prayer? His projected Wingdings loom above him like messengers from a different dimension. Despite the communication gap, he's got the most existentially soothing vibe I've ever encountered. The projected text strobes, an off-tempo light show.

He's gesturing to an avatar larger than the rest, a monument to pixelated vanity. It's 50% mullet, 30% hope, and the rest an antique high-school football picture. If I squint, it looks like it's crying.

The crew edges further into the maze. I double back to the monk. "Nice ambiance, right?" I say. "Real big. Real empty. Real - "

"✱✱✦✱✱✱✦✱," says the monk.

There are worlds of meaning in those marks. I catch something about spirits and failure, and make a note to ponder more deeply when it won't annoy me.

Syron's scanning holograms in rows of decaying avatar thumbnails. She doesn't give up easily. A shaky banner proclaims: GONE BUT STILL TRENDING. A lopsided fist bumps above.

"Stop screwing with your high score, Syron. We've got about thirty-six minutes until this place is wall-to-wall memory dumps."

"Like," says Syron, "thirty-seven, easy."

The abandoned CEO weeps some more, its tears and ego blurring with raw data. Half the ghosts are CEOs. The other half wanted to be. I know the type. Those who think the rules don't apply, and don't like finding out otherwise. People like me have to remind them. I nudge the monk again, less politely this time, and he falls in beside us.

We pass a floor-length motivational hanging. JITTERS MAKE THE BETTER QUITTERS. The smiley face emoticon stares into my soul.

Ahead, the calamari's got three tentacles deep in a dormant server cluster. The other five are swirling corrupted data like cyber-chantilly. A poem scrolls across its skin: Young suits fell down. / Broken, full of hope, they call / waiting for their chance. / Binaries buzz around it like gnats.

"Staying on task, System.Squid.AI?" I ask, risking distraction.

"Perception altered," it says in perfect haiku meter. It doesn't get annoyed, unlike certain other people I know. "Adjustments required. Tasks should reflect new contingencies."

If I were built like a sentient seafood salad, I'd say the same thing. I try not to take it personally, especially since it's usually right.

"Unloved echoes swarm," it says.

"Tell me something new," I say, dragging my thoughts out of their private tar pit. "We should move fast."

I step through more glitchy profiles, catching just a few words here and there. ENTITLEMENT TRAINER. INFILTRATED ANONYMOUS. WOULD LOVE TO CATCH UP! WHO KILLED MY CAT? HIRE ME, PLEASE?

It never ends, just flickers out slowly.

"Control is fluid," says the calamari. "Streams unpredictable. Slow but non-fatal."

"We only get paid if we deliver," I say. "Keep us moving, and it'll be like my cousin said: no worries." I pause. "That was right before they repossessed his jaw, but still."

We break left around a tower of blue-white corporate-lit

dreams. Ten thousand lumens of God Complex lighting, bored and blinking.

Syron holds back to grab more data. I signal to hurry. One hand taps the keys like a maestro on 8-bit meth, the other scrolls digital residue on a cracked tablet.

I'm wondering if I should just throw her over my shoulder and run, but I have my dignity.

Some dignity.

"Perception of time," says the squid, "differs based on life expectancy."

I glance back to see Syron a few feet behind me. "Told you," she says. "We have, like, forever."

Syron catches up. She's pulling my NeuroPoly carbon-hemor-rhoids-and-overhead for once. We're lucky if anyone here's remembered anything for years. Her hands work independent of her voice, circuit tattoos glistening beneath fraying sleeves. "Bro," she says, "this gig pays enough to turn even you corporate."

"It's easy money," I say, meaning it this time. "Once they find out you're here, they'll just surrender and die again."

"We could have just stayed at the IO, written everyone up as casualties, and billed the Corps out the wazoo," says Syron. She runs up beside me, watching her holographic trail and hacking new growth onto it. Not everyone lives with the same reckless regard for safety.

"I take a spiritual stand against simulation," I say. "My soul is clean."

The ghost of an exec with pinstripe echoes glitches past, uncommitted, like a tourist looking for Vegas and winding up in Des Moines. There's more where that came from. We're gonna be swimming in them.

"We're good," Syron says. "Totally fine. We make our mark on this rock pile before anything corporeal shows up."

Something runs through the circuitry like current. I want to say life, but that's what they don't have. Not quite life, then. Refusal to shut the hell up and let go.

My implants light up. A few icons only slightly more welcome than my own tapeworms blink red, then turn into question marks and smiley faces. Both icons and parasites are Syron's gifts to me.

Looks like we're hitting a sweet spot.

I don't want to jinx it, but I think we might pull this off.

The decor's depressing. Decades-old fonts scream FAILURE TO CONNECT. They flicker from dusty CRT monitors like horror movie confessions. Streaming obits and farewell posts bounce off cracked plastic and broken screen-glass. Eulogies fight for attention and lose. Mid-century wannabe thought leaders console each other in oblivion. VCRs. MiniDisc players. Tape backups. Piles of vintage tech smother the walls and floor, multiplying like retro viruses. The whole place has a doomsday-prepper vibe. My HazelTech™ implants crawl with age-old requests and fizzling pings as we pick our way down a narrow corridor.

“Looks like Hoarders R Us,” I say. The hardware is a sickness, spreading. "Probably left to upgrade themselves into sentience."

Syron’s at a wall-mounted console, finger-talking it through a crisis. Her sarcasm levels are nuclear.

"Found your kindergarten report card,” she says. “Solid *B*s. Good hustle."

“Careful,” I say. “I heard cardboard is bad for the environment."

The stuff bulks out around us in lean-to fortresses, sagging towers. One room even has a set of dumbbells. TEN TONS OF GLITCH, bulging like beefcake servers on steroids. The equipment gives up less hope than its owners.

An audio file crackles to life as we pass: “TELL SUSAN IT WAS ALL FOR HER.”

More of the same. So much history, so much to make it meaningless. This crew knows what it means to hang on that tight. Knows the agony of wanting to forget. We fit right in.

"Be careful out there, Susans of the world," Syron warns. "It’s gonna be a long winter.”

“Cold as your heart, you mean.”

It takes a pro to sound cheerful when every lead turns cold and every relationship turns transactional. We all find our talents.

Syron is talented as fuck.

A couple broken drones watch us like dull-eyed sheep. The monk floats one into life and taps a gentle pulse across its code shell. Subtle signals echo off metal walls as if he's trying to start a new religion.

"We lost track of a voice," the message says. "Goodbye." A quick transmission in any century. One I know too well. I tighten my jaw and press on. The screens flicker faster, louder. The signatures burn and fade.

No wonder I'm feeling hunted. HUNTERS HAVE EXCELLENT SELF-ESTEEM reads a three-meter fold-out banner. I'm developing my own, one line at a time.

The calamari reports in from a set of manual release levers. "Defensive configurations. Rapid collapse unlikely."

"We're not set for good news." Syron pauses, watching the disarrayed wires and overturned workstations like there's something deep, metaphysical in them.

"The boss says, try for one thing less likely," I say. "Dude's ready to patch when you are."

Syron grins, frantic as the remains of a reality-TV host: fresh-stretched but not fooling anyone. She uses every tactic to keep up. Or every drug.

"Data!" she says. "Life's answer to everything." Her hands don't even come close to freezing, although the rest of her systems will sooner or later.

The monk hums what might be ancient wisdom. Or Journey. Or just something on repeat.

I pass him, then pull him along. The lines of dark red text from old management brochures blaze across the walls. BRO / SEEKERS ARE NOT WELCOME HERE. Broken? He's surrounded by characters - suspended altars, incense trails. Unscheduled and exactly how he likes them. It all falls into patterns.

"More scope than faith?" I ask. He never takes me up on it, but I'm a persistent kind of guy. And kind of a guy who persists. Like everyone here.

The monk keeps sending them out there - Wingdings. Intentions. Fractals. Guitars.

Maybe the biggest difference between me and him is this: he thinks some other arrangement will take all of us in. I think there's nothing out there but letters marked "return to sender."

Syron manages the operation like it's got some life in it. "All this love and loss. Almost gives me hope."

"Even a drop would kill you," I say. "How about speed?"

"The kind without bandwidth?" She shakes her head. It turns into a loop, a hallucinatory confidence: the deeper we go, the more assurance that none of this, none of us, none of the drama's ever mattered. I know that vibe too. "You're missing the party," Syron says.

Corrupt data piles around her. But hey, everything's for sale. Even attention.

"Lost but not forgotten," I say. "Fun as an unmedicated apocalypse."

She shivers once and darts ahead of me, flipping a yo-yo trick before setting up at the next console. Once she knows there's a payoff, I'm on my own again.

She lives for this crap. She lives for whatever fills the silence.

It's anything but silent here. Feeds keep going, and going, and going. As long as the subscriptions. As long as the obsessions.

"WE REGRET TO INFORM YOU."

"ANOTHER FIVE SECONDS."

"THOUGHT WE HAD FOREVER."

The data channels stop short, update their farewell tours, and return as "failure to proceed" notices.

The notices are comforting, even more than my own personal Susan. The hazard lights flash: DUCK AND COVER. And above everything: DON'T QUIT YOUR NIGHTMARES.

I want this operation wrapped before it's not just vintage but ancient. I'm convinced I see actual bones.

"Sick of this train yet?" says Syron. "Isn't it kinda redundant for guys like us?"

"We stay in one place, the ex-boyfriends find us," I say.

"Dude," says Syron. "Where's the chase?"

"On."

We barely wait to sync. Untraceable shards scatter the ground and lodge themselves in boxes marked PLAN FOR RETIRE-

MENT. Old invoices double the inventory. It's surreal as fuck, an endless tide. We're close to cashing in. And they all know it.

The monk draws it out. No hesitations, no question marks. ✷✶✦✷.

He says we're in it forever. Says we're holding too tight. We get louder and longer and stay the same. We're one ancient gang of Wingdings.

He might be right. It's not my problem as long as we're paid for it. The chances of that are rising as fast as the headcount, which also rises.

Not bad, not good, and all us.

The calamari re-maps the zone, reciting metrics with a personal touch. "Disorganization creates belief in structured existence. Attention alters perception."

The last hour feels like two months. Feels like maybe we need the philosophy.

Feathery-tipped clusters of profile packs open, deep blue. But more than anything: losing at faith, and filling space like a family reunion gone bad.

“This is too sad for words," says Syron. “Nothing says we have to watch it."

She's not wrong. It's too sad for even LinkedIn. But there's a current running, and we're not the only ones catching it. More and more screens, more hardware, more familiar loss letters - all rising, all building toward a new collapse.

More living than when they started.

Enough to hit max nostalgia. Enough to remind us where we stand. And falling fast.

If there's a choice between irony and self-destruction, the decision is made.

Syron leaves a permanent smudge: "This is one big LinkedIn reunion, only nobody left the building."

She doesn't have to suggest that we move faster. We do.

SKELM.trial 22

FIND grep_heroic_legacy.sh ; Ancestral Knowledge Mining

Like Zeus blew up a RadioShack, the LinkedIn server farm blasts out prismatic light and questionable business advice. Data entrepreneurs scale firewalls instead of mountains. Updates chase their tails like eternal return was just another form of spam. We step through what seems like several planes of existence, my companions blurred and buffered by reality's own syntax errors. Troy is here, somewhere. His booming voice glitches through the scene before his form materializes, flickering between Trojan War hero and tech-bro avatar with NFT jewelry. "WAGMI!" he yells, the absurdity taking shape as he tells it. He used to be the world's best warrior, now he consults.

"What's that stand for?" Syron asks. "We Are Going to Make Iowa?"

"Indoctrination of Wage Addicts," the calamari says, crossing eight limbs with such eloquence that its nano-sensors practically hum.

"Sounds like this guy," Syron mutters, jogging ahead. Her form flashes between her hoodies' glitch art and the LED's manic pulse. I'm ten paces back, holding my ground against all the bright promises. Can this server cowboy really know where Penny is? He's tagged everywhere with rumors, with code that matches her movements. Now that I've caught him, will he just keep me in beta?

"What do you think, is Darby's goddess of wisdom hanging with Mister Spam Immortality here?"

"If true, the implications are infinite and contain the entire system," says the squid.

"If true, the logic loops are already infinite," I say, joining them on a transparent platform that spans several realities. Every inch of the virtual environment demands my attention, but I'm locked on the absurdity of Troy's reality-hacking, attention-wrangling genius. It takes one to find one, maybe.

"Probs just someone riding his cache," Syron says. "Told you he'd be off-key and spamming."

This from the junkyard oracle, this from the black-market Coder of the Lost. I believe her and not at the same time. I can't stop thinking that every step through this underworld's improbable syntax gets me one closer to knowing.

When we stop to buffer, my system status flashes ready, not ready, WAGMI, ready.

"I've got to know what Troy meant by" - Syron reads the glyphs - "Indie Underwear Auction."

The monk shrugs and crosses his legs mid-air. A huge, luminous grin grows from its edge pixels. The anarchist and I aren't buying it. "Penny's somewhere past this ram, not that guy," Syron says, hitching a shoulder. "Soon as she flashes that OS, your social experiment here will fold like wetware."

And I want to say *no, there's more to it*, like this hologram can't find closure.

"You," comes a voice from every server rack. And then there's Troy, endless in digital and mortal space.

"No mention of low-cost digital training?" I ask, as the alpha centurion appears to alpha all other alpha-ness into its core.

The former hero of the former world strides into range, flickering between godlike avatar and human hack with hoodies to spare. I can't tell if his confident advance is boldness or graphics processing. I want to tell him, *I feel you, man. I'm walking exactly that contradiction every day.*

Instead, I hang back with wide-open eyes. Syron's on full hackle and pulling closer, even as she mistrusts.

The high-res god brings it with pure pomp, until his claims are at epic scale. "I, the great and humble Troy, humbly declare myself great," he says. "Do my senses deceive, or has the radiant crew of the Lopsided Equation deigned to enter my demesne?"

"Either your sense of smell or reality," Syron says, waving him off with a shaky arm.

"We can smell this far," I say.

"Tell me, divine travelers, what wisdom-seeking pilgrimage brings you to the Digital Underworld?" A shake of his blockchain keychains makes the absurdity sound epic. I'm pulling words out of mid-air as they appear. This server is all about blue ocean biz and social displacement.

“It’s got a school,” Syron says, nodding to the glitch banners as they iterate the bargain.

Troy laughs and switches frames, growing buffer time with every boast. “Seekest thou the Next-Gen Growth by Garage Labs with Build-a-Deity Workshop? Nay? Then surely you come to me for my latest Blockchain Bonanza?”

“No refunds?” says Syron.

“No matter!” says Troy. “You shall have them all. You shall have immortality and education both! Why not the spoils of my latest NFT conquest? They contain many Trojan.gifs.”

Even my Coder of the Lost can’t bring herself to snort that off. The calamari sends haikus across its skin. First lines emerge from the vivid textscape of its subtle sarcasm:

Heroic save /

on bonus multi-buy. /

Thrice! O life is glitching out. The bizarre folds back onto the absurd, as every one of Troy’s selves declares supremacy.

His cultist hustlers may believe it. Maybe they can spam divine themselves into checking accounts. What I believe is that this unlooped hero is too big to fake.

“If Patroclus could see me now, my startup here would be the Iliad!”

His gesture, his gaze, the lighting - they all say I should be closer.

I stay back and give Syron a leg-up on doubt, knowing she'll think this savior-salesman of the Digital Underworld doesn't know about my immortal this-life crisis. I let her see all that indecision before I close the distance and call his buffer. He pauses from conquering his new world, casts a golden-hued glance, and follows with gestures from a prosumer hologram I don't believe yet.

Darby! comes a new array of signals. *Tell me!* he says. His invincible ego is as huge as its cracks, and I begin to see something beyond the code in all that posturing. I'm close enough now to see it all unravel.

It unravels with swagger and unravels with jokes and mostly with a pixel-bright self-delusion that the great humility of Troy is equal to the great size of Troy. My light-speed companion has to smirk this part in. "Whoa, I think it's running long and didn't quite make it to Troy's datacenter."

"Can this one-time hero assist a now-time you? Or do the strong silent type above" - he gestures to the calamari as it writes itself into flash drives - "determine your non-consumption based tactics?"

A single tentacle moves and rewrites the system. Others arrange complex networks around impossible graphs. It seems distracted by concepts so foreign that they even escape Syron's bio-interface ports.

"So modest this guy had to move to a new blockchain just to fit the file," she says, deadpan. "What's the consensus on your NFT of the long-gone wifey?" I see the spike of hope like she's wrapped my quest into a time-share of the soul.

“A Trojan wifey, you say?” A grand gesture; epic boom; his take on my problem has new beta users already. “Perhaps that genius in systems and proclivity in passions has united us once again! My eternal trophy.” He sells himself hard enough to mean it, which gives him a head start on me. My own immortal this-life crisis starts right here, just a few frames and dimensions short of Trojan genius and all its hardware. It starts as a nameless virus, a code injected: So, you’ve found Penny, too.

He keeps immortal cool while doubt rewrites my logic.

I was expecting him to leave me off the end-user license, but here it is: As you humans say, did you think you'd make it? Before it writes to firmware, I'm out.

How can he show that much loyalty and not have the clues? How can I show that much need and not have the trust? I'm on pause and thinking what it would mean if Penny's game, if Troy's trip, is to do this all day, every day.

Twelve years or seconds later, we’ve gone so far down the fiber that even my commitment is having doubts. It looks and smells like someone built a hyperbaric chamber for expired brands of optimism. There are so many memes per capita here that nothing sticks to anything else. Troy has me inside the promotional loop, his gestures broadcasting confidence and a glossy yet evasive professionalism. The soul of a growth marketer. The shoes of an influencer god.

My crew and my conviction are lagging way behind. Maybe they're following Troy's elusive path through six or seven metaphysical side trips, or maybe they're all an ad campaign I can't afford to believe in. I wonder if it's really a lifetime when the colors shift so fast. Troy spins, capturing my questions and writing new ones across every holographic surface.

“Perishable brands,” he says, adjusting to his uncertainty as smoothly as any pivoting founder, “are of no use to me. With data flows this strong, I won't perish in any quarter. All are invested.” He seems to need this story told. I'm in a position to hear him. He leaves no niche unsaturated. “They will sing my legend,” he says, the epic one-man band of his own immortality. I'm impressed by the insistence. His act is only slightly longer than his lifetime. “Or stream it live with Q&A and commentary.”

“If bandwidth allows,” I say, arms crossed against the massive rebrand.

“It's a big thing for you humans, yes? Not perishing? As I always told Patroclus, even dead, it is good to live forever!” Troy throws me an ancient grin before collecting it into modern increments of impression and engagement. I watch it all get archived and delivered to stockholders.

Every time it hits Troy's servers, my doubt seems less important than the risk of believing him. Maybe it's all just optimization and cover stories.

“Code the mighty, therefore,” Troy says, guiding my hesitant footsteps past more shifting symbols, “that they might scale.”

“You need this translation help from humans?”

“Help is exactly what the great humility of Troy requires. In fact, you're already part of the promo! There, under ‘emerging thought leaders.’”

Somewhere out of scope, Syron's reading his unsubtle pixels and glitching my subscription to Troy's ambition. Am I the only one on this mailing list?

My wayfarer from underworlds digital and emotional continues. "With nothing to measure, there is nothing to build," Troy says. "With nothing to build, there is nothing to break." I want to counter but I'm struck by the kind of tenacity that usually finds other words for this. The absurd. The deranged. The divine. Instead, I remember to close my mouth and listen.

His inventory is full. The old-fashioned gift of listening is sure to add twenty followers and a fraction of a percent in new volume, he predicts.

His self-appointed accolade of One Who Sees Troy says otherwise. It asks the only questions I can't afford to keep and can't afford to sell. What do I gain by denying it? What do I lose? The rewards of certainty, the hazards of risk? I already live that market, why not stay?

"Destruction is freedom. That which endures resists the brand!" Troy has truly achieved my attention now.

So much attention that I lose his focus and get pulled back into circles of timeless but redundant lights, brought to me by the noble and enduring content providers at Real Uptime™ and The Philosophy Garage. Maybe that time is only spent in silence, but to Troy, it's way too long and never long enough. A gigacycle passes, with me still lost in systems and meaning. Finally, he overclocks in. I call out from the rim, "Thought this was my eternal trophy too!"

But it is, Troy says. You've already heard this code.

The zeppelin and its stray data feed catch up to me where it all began, looking smug about it, having just met themselves in alternate timelines. I don't get the luxury. I get to stay the course.

The loop collapses when I feel his glow on my shoulder, gold like I should catch up or fall back in the mythos of such pixels. *Darby! I'm rewarded. Tell me!* His pure pixels blind my need, outflank my instincts. *Did you think you'd make it?*

It seems Troy never doubts his commitment. No risk of exceeding bandwidth. "Make it and more! Call the narrative a virus. I've outlasted worse than time."

I think I'm getting closer to that myth. His new trophy, perhaps, can even keep him honest.

"With me to help build your poly-theistic business, your empire will be like Amazon," I tell him. "An all-powerful but resentful ex?"

"Or did you expect a goddess of the microchip to outlast a god of the pivot?" he says, releasing me into new variables, old truths, and scaled-up uncertainty. Is it fame and the big promotion that they called to this subdomain? The divine hesitation of that which doesn't know what it wants?

We want the giant question mark as the logic of my goals implode. We just want you for these genius systems, its runs and passions. Even by growth metrics, did you think you'd make it?

Troy knows my competing mythologies and keeps writing them into release notes. The depth and the hopeless mortal statistics.

Finally, Syron, the monk, and I coalesce, with such wit as we mortals have: full penetration and low data rates, never!

I linger near a payload. Time unpacks. What does the nihilist write?

Surely his lost wisdom of Planck time, multi-pass, Wi-Fi don't believe? Troy the Goliath of Tech takes his specs and campaigns into phase two, possibly overconfident in our lifetime.

With as much doubt as the marketing allows, I run Darby.exe to exceed expected durations. What did you expect?

SKELM.trial 23

DEL rm_-rf_pastlife ;
Cultural Memory Erasure

I stand in the neon glow of the digital console when my mother's avatar materializes in jagged pixels across the interface, her features both familiar and unnervingly distorted. The avatar's lips move as it asks, "Why you never call?" while my hazel eyes, glistening with reflections of data streams, narrow in disbelief. I fumble with the control panel, my fingers twitching against the slick surface, as the sudden intrusion forces me to confront a past I've long tried to forget. The ambient hum of circuitry and distant drone sirens intensify the moment, marking the start of my internal crisis, while my heartbeat thumps visibly in my temples. My defiant jaw sets; the room's neon flickers in time with my resolve as I ready myself for the decisive act to come.

The glow of holographic advertisements seeps in through cracks in the walls, casting prismatic shadows that mimic the glitching apparition on the screen. She looks like she used to in Iowa, before tech and time fractured our family into individual units of isolation. Now she's pixelating into memories I thought I'd erased, pieces of her flickering against the data streams that never stop flowing in this place.

"Darby," she says, stretching my name into a warbled moan, part accusation and part lament. I hate that she sounds so real. I hate that she even found me here.

My finger hovers over the control panel, and I want to feel nothing, to be indifferent to the past as she once was to me. But my hands shake, the slick console refusing my command as I fail again to shut her down. I hear the distant echo of a broken childhood ricochet through the digital void, striking me like shrapnel in a war I no longer wish to fight. The thin line between virtual and real space erodes, and I'm a kid again, trapped between her sadness and my longing to be elsewhere.

I pound my fist on the interface. The console flashes a garbled error message that stutters through my skull, amplifying my frustration. "Call your mother," she says. "If you're not too busy with that fancy reality of yours." Her face glitches, alternates between neglect and disappointment, then resets into a fractured smirk. The irony of this pixelated guilt trip would amuse me if it weren't slicing open wounds I thought had healed.

The avatar twitches, freezes for a second, then resumes her loop, the broken record of her question taunting me in low resolution. "Why do you never call?" This time, I hear a cruel parody in her voice, as if she knows exactly how desperate I was to get away and how well I've succeeded. My stomach knots with the familiar pressure of her need and my failure to meet it. I'm on the edge of a past I can't hack my way out of, her jagged fragments multiplying across the screen like an unwelcome virus.

I push back from the console, my movements jerky with unresolved tension. The ambient noise grows louder, the circuit board hum climbing in my ears, colluding with her image to break me down into emotional subroutines. My head pulses with the pressure of remembering, each beat of my heart rendered in the same cold pixelation as her endless "Darby, Darby, Darby," unraveling me in binary guilt. She's no more tangible now than she was in our living room, but somehow, that makes it worse. She's everywhere at once, and I am nowhere.

"Answer me, Darby," the avatar says. It shouldn't hurt, but it does. Maybe more than it should. I'm still the runaway, still the selfish kid in her eyes. I have to cut this off before she's all I see.

This time, my jaw clenched tight, I reach again for the DELETE key. But the console, like my memory, refuses to comply. She lingers, even when she shouldn't. Especially when she shouldn't. I collapse into the nearest chair, letting my fists go limp, hoping for numbness that won't come.

My eyes burn as they trace her pixelated outline. I almost laugh. Of course she'd find a way to haunt me, even here, on the LED Zeppelin, the one place in the universe I thought I was safe.

The room glows its silent accusation as I struggle to override my emotions, the same way I've overridden my entire life up to now. The screen strobes with each attempt I make to relegate her to memory. But nothing deletes. Nothing ever deletes.

I squeeze my eyes shut against the flashing lights, against the hurt that's found me here. I wait for it all to go dark, for her to finally disappear. But when I open them, she's still there, all pixels and loss, floating against the electric hum of everything I tried to leave behind.

She glitches one more time, the sad phantom of a mother insisting on being seen. My anger trembles into something I don't want to name, my heartbeat a neon drum in the distance between us. I won't let her do this again.

Resolve steadies my fingers. *She's not real*, I tell myself, and this time, I almost believe it. She never was. This time, I know exactly how to end this. I know exactly what to do.

With a rapid swipe across the holographic interface, I execute the deletion protocol on my digital account, each keystroke accompanied by a burst of electric sparks that momentarily camouflage my twitching features. The account severs, the screen abruptly displaying a stuttering void that embodies my symbolic break from the past. In the background, my crew assembles - Syron tapping furiously at a vintage keyboard, the vat-grown calamari sliding across the deck with a fluid grace, and the nihilist monk unintelligibly punctuating the air with Wingdings-laden exclamations. They clink their improvised glasses, shouting, "Living fast, dying never!" as they collectively hack into the obituaries, their actions punctuated by rapid-fire commands and the occasional irreverent snort. The scene bursts with kinetic energy and digital chaos, solidifying my momentary catharsis while the crew's ensuing celebration blurs the line between anarchy and rebirth.

I watch my account disappear with a little sigh that sounds a lot like "Darby." My hands stop shaking. My heart decelerates from rave tempo to acoustic strumming. It's over. I am free of her at last.

The console flashes a few last reminders of the moment we lost each other. I delete those too. I delete until nothing is left, not even my own code, and it feels like the first inhale after holding my breath for seventeen years. I'm alone with my friends. We aren't friends, but maybe we are. Who knows? Not me. Not the runaway.

The stuttering void tells me I have no messages, and for once, I believe it. My shoulder drops, shedding the weight of family obligation and all those words she tried to reach me with. Goodbye, Mother, and good riddance. She won't care. I won't care. I won't let myself.

"Surprise!" says the squid, tickling me with a tentacle and holding an unopened bottle of ethyl surprise, our favorite way to forget we're already forgotten. I give it a long pull, feeling my hard edges soften with the cheap burn of oblivion. My head clears, just enough to start confusing the void in my chest for freedom.

"Man of the hour!" Syron shouts. She swivels her oversized headphones like old-time radio mics and grins at me from the console next door. Her eyes do the same sad lightshow mine do. "How does it feel to have a warranty again?" she asks, fingers sprinting across her stolen QWERTY. "New account smell?"

I tell her it smells a little like empty, and she gives me a thumbs up paired with a smile that says *empty is what we're all after anyway*. She cracks open the box to another keyboard and hands me a shotgun hack. The words "live wires" dance across the display.

The crew gets ready to drink the night until it buffers. Syron uses her visual synthesizer to patch up some instant memories, flickering low-res stills of last year's bender, that weekend it took me a week to piece together. I want to remember it better this time, want to feel that careless without the drone of her distant affection slowing my jam. I let my arms remember how to dance. I let myself believe we are a perfect loop of electric now, my friends and me.

The LED Zeppelin hums like a ready amp as the monk fills his lungs with oxygen and nihilism, spewing lines of existential gospel into the empty space we call our own. They are all in Wingdings, but I get the point: detachment is a state of mind. If they are happy, it doesn't matter. If I'm not, that doesn't either.

Syron writes me an obituary on the fly. It reads: "Boy. Deleted." She kisses me on the cheek, and I short-circuit like it's my first crash, feeling everything go weird and awkward, feeling it fizzle down my nervous system in sloppy jumps. The whole room grins at me like she meant it, like this could be another new beginning. I raise my glass and pretend she did.

The squid puts its ethyl surprise down long enough to man the ship. It steers with a cold eight-pack of flailing certainty, navigation lights flashing in binary code to let me know it's got the helm, it's got my back, it's got haiku if I need some poetry with my rebirth.

"Just like family," says the monk, and the words hang over the deck like the bad trip they never were, something none of us ever wanted to escape. I think of Mom, I think of Dad; I think I can't let myself think these things.

"Look, Ma," I say to the void. "No attachments!" And I spin until everything's a warm blur, until there's no sadness to my softening edges. My mother's image is gone but I still hear her. I wonder if I ever won't.

The crew forms a closed circuit of blurry smiles. We stay that way until our laughter is one corrupted file, until we forget what we were running from, until nothing matters except how we keep on dancing.

SKELM.trial 24

JZ navigate_binary_choice.fork
; False Dichotomy Creation

The trick to not getting digitally eaten is pretending you belong, even when every pixel of reality hates your meat. It's the same old mall food court trick: keep moving, don't stare at the currency exchangers, try not to trip on your own pants, and above all - never admit you want out.

I ghost into the IO.wav market node at triple overlay. The grid pops me in low and tight at "street" level, except here, the street is a drunken Möbius strip of light-cube vendor stalls, suicide alleys, and currency dropboxes disguised as morphing fauna. Holo-adverts detonate above me in blue-orange shudders: Are You Earning Enough Attention? Swap Your Sleep Debt For Status! Limited-Time Kink Subsidies! Synthetic bass rolls like thunder up the walls of old data, buzzing at frequencies engineered to scrape the plaque off your hypothalamus. Smells like burnt cotton candy and ozone.

The map says the Admiral is somewhere in the wet end of the plaza, but "somewhere" is a physical impossibility here. Every vector wants to fold you backwards, split you sideways, pop your organics into the entropy river. My HazelTech™ retinal mods flex, refocusing with a little serotonin pulse as I force my eyes to follow the strobing arrows. I can already see the Admiral's financial signature leaking into the crowd, flagrant as a pheromone spill.

But first, the sideshow. Syron, my unofficial handler, keeps pace at my left elbow, arms crossed in self-defense and jaw set in a sardonic parabola. She's running the same reality filter as me, but with the gamma cranked up so everyone glows slightly radioactive.

"See the CEO?" Syron mutters, just loud enough to parse through my left auditory canal.

I nod. "Smells like fresh blood and botulism. She's shadowing the flex booths."

"Probably has ten backups in every vector." Syron is visibly restraining herself from flipping off the nearest DebtHound™ drone as it circles us, broadcasting sub-audible reminders to Stay Current, Stay Secure, Stay Sane.

"Don't engage the drones," I warn. "We're already tagged."

Her mouth jerks sideways, somewhere between a smirk and a snarl. "Bro, in this town even the air is tagged. If you're not on five lists you don't even have a pulse."

Behind us, the rest of our party pretends not to exist. The sentient vat-grown calamari glides, gelatinous and nearly invisible, by subtle undulation of its nano-fiber cilia. Only when it shifts to avoid a phasing trolley do I spot the bio-luminescent status code flickering through its arms: "probing / assessing / poised." The Nihilist Monk - today wearing an orange-on-orange robe with USB tassels - drifts behind the cephalopod, hands clasped and eyes slightly rolled. His head glows with the dim, contemplative blue of a Brainwave Economy addict. Together they make the world's worst parade.

"Found her," Syron mutters, snapping a wetware ping straight into my optic nerve. The Admiral occupies a vendor dais at the center of the plaza, surrounded by holographic survival guides, riot insurance kiosks, and - because it's Tuesday - a flock of livestreaming gulls made of pure monetized outrage. The CEO has a face made of spliced memory: square and reliable but impossible to focus on for longer than a second. Each time I look at her, she is reconfigured to optimize trust and admiration.

The crowd parts for her in programmed waves. She's got two suit-clones for flanking (identical but for their ties: one pale pink, one gold), and every fourth second, a third "follower" instance boots up behind her, lingering just long enough to be seen before winking out again. The Admiral slaps a digital contract onto the translucent negotiation slab and waves us forward with a gloved hand.

We walk the gauntlet like doomed contestants on a game show called Is Your Data Worth Dying For? I imagine my hair slick with sponsorship, my skin laminated with product placement. In reality, I'm sweaty, hungry, and about one minor breakdown from punching the next person who tries to sell me neural malware as a dietary supplement.

The CEO greets us with her best "I'm definitely a real person" smile. "Welcome to the Admiral's Bazaar, where every deal is a lifeline," she says, voice set to comfort but leaking menace in the harmonics.

I force my own smile. “We’re looking for survival. In bulk.”

A flicker of teeth. “Aren’t we all?”

She gestures at the negotiation slab, where the contract is already rendered in living code. The words pulse and twist, never the same arrangement twice. Reading it directly would be like staring into a strobe light, so I let my mods translate.

“You’ll be wanting the Platinum Scream package,” the Admiral says, sliding the document toward me. “Covers all civil unrest scenarios, economic disintegration, spontaneous quantum-local genocide events, and, of course, long-term spiritual debt.”

“Spiritual debt?” Syron interrupts, lifting an eyebrow. “Is that an upsell, or just a threat?”

“Why not both?” the CEO purrs. “The latest models of Debt-Hound™ are fully equipped for soul balance collection.”

Syron’s hands go in her pockets. I feel the tremor in her right arm, where the skin barely conceals the homemade patch array beneath. I nudge her foot under the table: steady.

The Monk projects a string of Wingdings across the slab: ✹✶✦✳. The CEO’s suit-clones read it and instantly freeze. The code is untranslatable to my mod, but I recognize the freeze as a sign of deep processing.

The calamari, finally visible for the moment, slides a tentacle up onto the slab and delicately probes the contract’s logic chain. Where the CEO’s fingers moved with economy and violence, the calamari’s are pure grace - flipping lines of quantum code, testing the knots, occasionally inserting a haiku into the margin. I sense the negotiation going both above and below my bandwidth.

"The Monk says the terms are recursive," I say, hoping to hurry this along.

"Not recursive," the Admiral objects, "elegant. Reality is self-correcting. The cycles are a feature, not a bug."

The tentacle stirs, flicks, and in the sub-text, an error blossoms: an infinite loop of tiny monochrome seppuku emojis. The Monk hums, quietly, a note that makes my fillings vibrate.

I exhale and lean forward, giving the CEO my full attention. Her suit-clones unfreeze, then double in number - now four in a row, blinking in synchronized rhythm. "We want option three," I say.

"There is no option three," she says, but the contract in front of us rewrites itself. It starts to leak blacklight from the edges.

"I'm guessing Tin Eel will disagree," Syron says. She's right: across the plaza, a ripple of muttering and low-grade panic marks the arrival of the competition. Tin Eel is less a CEO than a glitch in the happiness matrix, all pointy teeth and serotonin subscription pop-ups. Her approach is less direct, more viral - infecting bystanders with a contact high that tastes like warm plastic and forgiveness.

In less than a minute, the two predator queens are facing off across the negotiation slab. Admiral, in brute-force authority mode, and Tin Eel, slithering through the gaps of consensus.

Admiral speaks first. "Your presence here is redundant. The negotiation is concluded."

Tin Eel overlays the table with a refractive ripple of her own contracts, each written in language designed to short-circuit desire: "Accept Bliss Now," "Surrender Want," "Choose Happy." The surface of the table can't decide which universe to obey.

"It's an open market, Admiral," Tin Eel says. Her voice is a blend of synthetic comfort and the echo you get in your ear when you're about to pass out. "Our friend here is entitled to explore all available outcomes."

"Your offers are always hallucination in a pretty wrapper," the Admiral sneers. "Mine is the only solution with a future attached."

"And your future is always pain, delivered with a smile," Tin Eel counter-purrs.

The tension is so thick it could gel and pour over pancakes.

My mods say that both offers are fundamentally traps, but I already knew that. One is agony with a bulletproof exit plan. The other is ecstasy until the floor drops out and you find yourself hollowed. The only certainty is that neither side allows bystanders. You are either in or you are fodder.

I weigh the offers, or at least pretend to. Syron's hands twitch. The calamari flicks out a poem in its chromatophores: "Decision / is the virus / Truth in the divide."

The Monk flicks another string of Wingdings that I, for once, can almost read: a sequence of arrows pointing simultaneously at both CEOs and then, cryptically, at the contract slab itself.

I get it. The trick is not to pick. The trick is to play for time, let the predators fight, and hope the chaos creates a space where real choices can happen.

“Let’s see the terms,” I say, my best game show voice.

Both CEOs grin, a microsecond out of sync. The contracts bloom open, side by side. Syron leans in and starts to cross-analyze, lips moving silently as her mods scrape the fine print for viruses and brainworms.

Tin Eel’s contract is temptingly gentle, promising “complete satisfaction” with minimal side effects. The table begins to reek of dopamine and ripe stone fruit.

The Admiral’s offer is all protection and punishment, guarantees written in unbreakable code. A faint odor of iron and disinfectant pulses from her contract. I read the death clause, the pain thresholds, the “automatic pain audit.” My skin tries to flinch away, but the table’s haptic field holds me locked in.

In the periphery, a dozen DebtHound™ drones close in, emitting a low whine tuned to the frequency of financial panic. The bystanders start to melt away. The stage is set.

“Make your choice,” both CEOs intone, voices perfectly overlapped.

Behind me, the Monk hums louder. The calamari vibrates with anticipation. Syron gives me a hard, flat look, one I know means, “If you’re going to do something stupid, now’s the time.”

I smile, and - just for a second - I feel like I belong here.

“Okay,” I say, grabbing the negotiation slab in both hands, and wait for the moment both predators lean in. It’s always in the hesitation. The fractional tick when predators compete, and the prey stops playing the game.

I slam the contracts together. Holographic code detonates in a shower of half-formed legalese and error messages. The digital air howls, the slab reboots, and the room glitches sideways - catapulting all of us into the emergency arbitration layer, a blank white nothing lined with infinite slabs.

For a moment, there is only the pulse of my own blood in my ears, the cold shimmer of possible outcomes. I feel the biometric field tighten around me: it wants a signature, a yes or no, a surrender to the binary.

I refuse.

So do Syron, the calamari, the Monk. All at once, we drop our collective presence into a state of indefinite non-commitment, holding at the edge of decision like gods on a cigarette break. The two CEOs, starved for resolution, begin to cannibalize each other's contracts, clauses dueling, warranties shredding, until neither offer is even theoretically valid.

It only lasts a second. But a second is all I need to see the future crack open, to catch the glimpse of a way through.

"You're insane," Syron mutters, but there's admiration in her tone.

In the glitch-rain of collapsing options, I reach out and grab her hand.

And together, we run the corridor of pure Maybe, dodging the jaws of hungry binary, the scent of dopamine and rust, until we burst out the other end into a new, formless market square - clean, bright, and just barely ours.

Until the next predator finds us.

But for now, my pulse is my own.

Somewhere inside the endless reset, the market square regrows itself: columns of daylight shotgunned through clouds of pixel fog, ad-carts rebooting with amnesiac chirps, the whole floor tiled with the fractal afterimage of the last crash. My hand is still fused to Syron's. The moment freezes in the white-limbo lag you get when reality's core routine reboots but the wetware running it just wants to puke.

"You broke the contract slab," Syron says. Her voice is reverent, shaky, and ten percent homicidal. "Do you have any idea what that costs?"

I blink, and my mods show the aftereffects. The Admiral is nowhere, at least not where she's supposed to be. Tin Eel has collapsed into a million feral pop-ups, all fighting for attention with increasingly desperate offers: Eternal Contentment, Endless Afterglow, Click Here For Meaning. None of them land. The haptic field is busted, spitting out static.

But someone is still here. In the center of the new marketplace, floating in a shadow-puddle of blue-black, is the calamari.

Before, it tried to look invisible: rolling with the crowd, flickering out of focus. Now, it glides across the pixel tile like a cathedral's holy smoke, every step measured in code-pure geometry. Its body is a glass bell jar full of lightning. The tentacles reach, unhurried, and lay claim to the only thing left that matters: the negotiation slab's core logic, now a raw spindle of live quantum code pulsing in the center of the square.

The cephalopod hovers there, not touching but almost. The air around it prickles, taste of conductive gel and raw sodium. At first, it does nothing. Then it begins to move, each arm composing a sequence of gestures that even my top-tier mods can't parse. It's hacking, but not like any hack I've seen. No brute force. No code-injection. This is ballet.

Syron's nails bite into my wrist. "Watch," she whispers.

I do.

The first tentacle strokes the logic spindle, reading its surface. The code responds: rippling, fragmenting, briefly coalescing into a screaming face that is equal parts Admiral and Tin Eel. The face opens its mouth, but the sound is cut off by the second tentacle, which taps the base with perfect, metronomic rhythm - bypassing every digital tripwire and legal fail-safe. A third tentacle, iridescent with a curl of poetry, unfurls and overlays the spindle with a spectral map: routes out, roads not even on the nav. The spindle starts to come apart, logic segments disconnecting and recombining in new, impossible ways.

Suddenly, the system panics.

Binary code cascades down every visible surface, screaming for a restart. The lights go ultraviolet. Drones re-manifest, now flayed open to reveal the rotting, corporate code beneath. Everything in the square gets sucked into a recursive loop, sucking more and more until the whole thing folds inward, right down to the calamari.

It doesn't resist. Instead, it opens itself: expands its mantle until it covers the logic core, filters every byte of malicious code through its own chromatophores, and then - it sings.

The sound isn't sound. It's a wave, washing through every interface at once. I feel it in my stomach, the root of my tongue, in the tiniest bones of my skull. It's the opposite of a crash; it's a reset as primal chant.

On my overlays, a line of poetry blooms. It's a haiku, pure and without owner:

Virus eats the root,

but the fruit remembers light.

Divide. Compile. Run.

The logic core, now swaddled in cephalopod embrace, pulses once and explodes - this time, not in chaos but in clean, cool silence. No code. No contracts. Not even the smell of dopamine.

For a breathless moment, the world has zero rules.

In the vacuum, I turn to Syron. Her lips are moving, but there is no sound. She's laughing, or maybe crying, or both.

The Monk stirs beside me, his saffron robe fluttering like a flag at the edge of the void. His LED scalp pulses fractal green, and he projects a simple line of Wingdings into the air:

✸✶✦✳ - freedom.

I find myself grinning, wide and foolish, for the first time in years.

Then the world collapses back, pixel by pixel, but now it is ours. The CEOs are gone. The market square is wild, untamed, with a hundred emergent deals flailing in glorious disarray. Every rule, every exploit, every ban on the books - all gone or up for grabs.

I grab Syron and spin her around, because now there is nothing left to lose. The Monk laughs, the calamari ripples, and in the rebirth, we are suddenly, beautifully, free.

Which lasts about thirty seconds, before the next Debt-Hound™ slithers out of the undercode and sounds its first, uncertain note. But this time, it's different. This time, I am ready.

I square up to the drone, and smile with all my teeth.

Let the predators come.

SKELM.trial 25

NUL 404_toenail_not_found.haiku
; Deliberate Obscurantism

The underworld crumbles behind us, but LED keeps ahead of the falling sky, each fragment a bruised reminder of data once owned. The thing's mostly yellow now and crackling like cheap electricity, bruising my irises with sickly blue. Lines of stray code evaporate above us as we drift past, detaching and collecting like bad wiring. The cargo bay glows against the bright nothing we've surfaced into. And now, Admiral and Tin Eel look stranded as LED's systems go digital exorcist, bleeding possession across the boards.

"This calls for System.Squid.AI," Syron says, refusing to say more. Flash and cut from thin screens of glitch fill every surface and are now rolling like a tide toward land. "Error 404 / The sea was never silent / Refund your toenails," taunts the one-upping haiku as their offices sink out of code. Tin Eel emits a nauseous whimper. Admiral stiffens and grows six additional backs. ✸✶✦✳ twitches and hangs meditatively still from the cable rapture.

Digital galleons. Sea monster bling. Even letters sell out on deck as corporate ensigns catch in red glitch frames. Syron narrows her eyes and mumbles an erasure poem of noise, the smug commitment of a signature: *It. Is. Finished.* Below her, I just float through and wonder about horizons.

The sky stacks itself in a mess of everything; blues and greens file for compensation under yellow legal pads, rival shifts filling bankruptcy's blind spots. Neon decisions run to gaps in purple alibis, chaos seeking calm like victims on Crimewatch.

He's holding up pretty good, our chaos, until System.Squid.AI mans up and gets hostile. Then, its dump begins: torrents of death-release forms, shipping unchecked from six identical outlets. The floor keeps catching bytes it can't handle, throwing back version control errors that fill our feed. We ride it out as hot code shakes itself into particle condition, packing itself small in cycles. Fractals call out redundancies and cut all threats at digital slits. Most cycles decompile on entry, some panic into exile at street level.

Syron is savoring her anti-futures as I tune them from past to perfect. ✱✱✦✳ taps monk anagrams in flickering type.

THE MIST / BROKE A / JUMP CUT

It happens without restraint. Now, Admiral and Tin Eel are victims, full recipients in pieces. Possession eats their feed-back until silence is toxic and all ends download. I lean as we've gained; landlocked now are bodies (either fallen or grounded).

We're free; the past sinks slowly. Our gains unfold from comfort chairs. We breathe the colored scheme. They play with glitch leaves overhead, call it gone, and dismiss overtime.

The digital afterlife suffocates us. Our rapture is set to a hymn of glitch, the pace too rapid for immersion in systems other than breakdown. Between distant colors we still detect intent: profit in neon casts, its dead light filtering even here. By now, it's licked us empty with terminal confessionals, bites of static mumbled and bland. From humble connections to perjury, we testify our own account of dust: wireless / is the / breath of God, says the least holy, ✸✶✦✳. Is it just this when we crash? One big download? Less transaction than I expected, less gain and more reduction - a cache of none. “It could all come / from the home / office,” says the blue.dot.corporate under System.Squid.AI. How much is there before endgame?

The zeppelin’s frame rattles its outline of panic against chaos and sends it to us by direct linkage. Some connections prefer silent mode: the corpse of bio with digital bloat for weight and a gravitational marker in cyan: MyKarma_Overdraft.exe, infers the background. Limbo is a warehouse. Heaven just runs itself. “Can you believe in what doesn't matter,” I want to know - life, so hopelessly composed?

“It's memos all the way down,” says System.Squid.AI in brash relief. Our update reaches full confusion.

“Maybe you have to live it,” says Syron, the sound so cheap it hurts; she can never shut it down.

I poke at control panels flashing with insistence and bogus subscriptions. There has to be more to digital than leftovers, more to crash than empty nests. You think the bytes outlive the code? Does the network go beyond itself?

“The key / to being / the keys,” says the false prophet in symbols of strength. Absolution skips a frame.

TO: Whom / FROM: Your Future / I'm Not, Syron finishes our excuse on the least lines possible. How did we end / or are / we not / done?

✱✶✦✳ is getting churchy with binary design; humming syntax fills the errors like creed. Set up like this, we've got religious coverage, last rights in three networks. Even plastic replicas of the faithless provide comfort. Does it mean anything, Syron?

“We trail you / in sales,” says the arm of the dubious law; 48.PTS returns to 2. They planned this. Now it's corrupt deliveries, post ex-rapture. Neon packets carelessly resume the duties of promotion.

Get enough abandon and something's bound to work, they say. Not less in words or data. *Another flood in time,* I hear from somewhere remote, some cynical extreme.

If bytes exist, what's one more stream?

Nothing left to order.

We ran out on claims.

Can you make it?

I shrug. There's time.

Reality slips in from the wet. It dries out under the light, context quickening to declare it true. The digital in box sets, box as the store front, sets as inevitable. Reality spills at full market, concedes nothing as less.

Wireless or, confides the ⓏⒶⒾ® you.sweatshop / belief.at, it still / keeps.

SKELM.quest 6

STR io.wav ; The Compile of Reality

SKELM.trial 26

AUTH ssh_anarchist_favela.key ; Homecoming Protocol Subversion

The scene reboots itself repeatedly as we land - infinite kaleidoscopic variety packed into infinite tiny parcels, for all eternity, on sale now. A thousand maps cycle past, each one claiming to be the last, as the buildings and sidewalks reconfigure, swerving between existence states. Buy one reality, get ten free. Pick your favorite flavor of ephemerality. I don't like any of them. They're all spam. The crew's only slightly less ephemeral than the scenery, though I'd like to think we're a bit better at knowing where we're going.

It's like watching evolution in fast forward. Bright things grow out of nowhere, mutating through bizarre digital Darwinism until they implode from their own insanity. Structure becomes abstraction becomes confetti becomes dust. I squint, and the scene de-reses in one more desperate flash. Somewhere, some overworked, underpaid code monkey has a mental breakdown. Next frame, please.

The ground struggles with its own commitment issues. It's a gritty cement slab, an undulating network of digital runes, a comfy-cushy quantum error. It's a confession: none of the above. We're too many gigabytes and a decade late for this place. The locals know it; their side-eye glances pulse with disdain as we jump through the next erratic doorway.

"Nice reboot cycle!" I shout at one passing blur. "Where'd you steal it?"

"Nice implant," crackles a retort. "Where'd you sell out?"

At least my RetScans don't glitch out with every microsecond of change. I've been around enough freakish places to know the mental uninstall process, to stay five thought cycles ahead. Code flickers into scaffolding, blink into bricks, blink into what-the-hell-was-that. I exhale slowly, drop back to philosophical root access, and leave my adrenal settings on idle. Adaptation's a survival instinct in these sectors. There's no such thing as stability in a one-night-stand with physical reality. Good thing we're not here to stay.

The crew's a neon cut-out of absurdity against absurdity. Nihilistic software monks with Wingdings souls. Sarcastic genesplicers, rogue AI packs, little realities that didn't quite meet the manufacturing specs. We're more deranged tangos than lost souls. We'd like to think so, anyway. The signal noise keeps trying to convince us otherwise.

We slip through alleys more ethereal than actual - paths through fibrous knotwork of distorted bytes and tangled cord. Reality derails and re-enrolls, scattered files against an imaginary deadline. Code, construct, obsolescence, restart. Am I having fun yet? "Whee!" I say. "This is better than a barrel of cocaine-coded cyber-monkeys."

"Sarcasm is the bandwidth of a compressed mind," says a glowing cluster of philosophized circuits.

"Sarcasm is our guiding life force," I say.

The Styrofoam gods of glitch offer up their muted versions of Zen. None of it surprises me. Not anymore. I've floated between too many abandoned sectors to mistake them for stability. I can process change at clock cycle speeds. I can play hopscotch on dying memories and expired databases. At the end of the recursive string, I still know the file path we're meant to find.

Exocortex-wild sigils give way to corroded cement gives way to void. Local anarchists fragment like the looped sounds they live for. A nested loop, and another. I'll skip a few; I'll skip one; I'll skip none. As many as it takes to meet my target spec. "An entirely human instinct," a small irony says, "but well enhanced." A gossamer collective of code mumbles noncommittally into itself, creates consensus, uncreates consensus, becomes probability, perhaps.

We're only missing the lawn gnome. There, it mocks me in seventeen colors. There, it leers in gray. The utility fog embraces its contradictions with admirable defiance. Fractal walls and perceptual handshakes argue amongst themselves and lose the argument every time.

No straight lines. No stable corners. Layers and hallucinations crashing against each other like some frenetic digital orgy. We brush by fast-breathing cyber squatters, living-experiments-gone-bad, then watch them come into existence and unexist again. My data filters sweep their crazy presence, but I stay two compressions out. I'm philosophical, man. I'm every nihilist prophet's future hero, pixelated.

Said prophets mutter jokes from inside simulation loops, splicing texts from epigrams to cyber-Bibles. They preach bandwidth and generosity, and I don't know what else. They seem glad to hear us passing. Maybe it relieves them. They couldn't handle more variables.

"No extra syntax, thanks. I've already compiled. Maybe next millennium?"

"Haha. Haha."

Who's the junkies and who's the dope? Biochip babies yell binary epiphanies. Cool patches of electromagnetic scent leak from duct-taped cinderblocks, sniff at our bad avatars, shrug, try again, and shrug. In-the-know icons have already redecorated their status. They've moved on to fresher hacks. They glitch across my field of view, expecting me to care, to update my OS. No such luck. I'm there. Then I'm not. My one file is already in the transfer buffer, and I am as spam and ignore lists made me.

We're building anticipation through redundancy, suspense through recursion. I'm closing on Penny - dear, elusive glitch-genius Penny - through a billion exponential dead ends. And then: not. A sub-second time to never.

She's good at not existing in any place for too long. That's why I'm the one here now. We'll see who's laughing at the final pass.

. . .

You could argue that any coder here is alone, in the vast, infinitely recursive sense, but there's a little anarcho-chic tattoo in the far corner that definitely, singularly, almost angrily belongs to her. Reality parses around her in concentric contradictions. Solitude in the least solitary sense of the word. Penny. The mods are impossibly impressive, but I'm not here to appreciate the latest iterations. A direct approach isn't quite how we usually play these games, but I beeline anyway. She sees me before I hit breakpoint proximity. A single-line loop: close that open door.

Ten-thousand-decoders-trapped-in-a-digital-lounge dialogue throws its syntax in my direction, more a challenge than a welcome. She must be five nested code states away, but it might as well be a universe. Her recompiled laughter comes with a deadline: Are you even trying, or is it only coincidence?

I'm trying. More than she'll admit. I push through arrays of programmatic lives all hitting peak compile at once. Misfit manifestations and half-baked hardware hack jobs. Counter-culture cliques and cyber commies throw back their itinerant confessions in exabytes of audio and data. "Jabberwock's third law of applied realities!" one dazed collective says. "Avoid nouns or at least regret them immediately!"

How anarchist-core. Everything subroutine-yet-somehow-critical explodes in whimsical fanfare and dying function calls. They're the centerpiece of their own malcontent reality, still warm and writhing from the philosophical oven. The syntax echoes through my bandwidth. Convergence never gave me that particular hard-on. But maybe Penny, for all her resistance, remembers exactly what the new-age missionary had to offer.

In three more data pools, in two more reincarnated concrete structures, I'm nearly there. I glance around for sub-quests and minor distractions - anything but the focus that still surprises me after all these abandoned schemas. There's only noise and fervent noisemakers, and they all collapse away from her as they redefine themselves. Her conspicuous form gets even more conspicuous. A schema of singularity: revision 23.0.

Now I'm doing the impossible, the impatient, the now-or-never. I subroutine the space between us into irrelevance. Prox, but not as prox as I thought. Twenty years of untested algorithms in between. "✸✶✦✳," says a symbol-drenched post-entity as I pass, pronouncing the Wingdings with a grin. Its manifesto T-shirt adds, in a bold decompiling font, "EVOLVE YOUR CODEBASE."

Somehow, Penny's figured out a way to loom even while hunched over the unstable servers she commandeers. Outlines and cables jut in fourteen artistic directions. She's sampling fresh code from living streams, hitting real-time remix levels I've never seen. She's coded impossibly hard this time, but who hasn't? The awkward embrace or cold departure waits between us. I stop pretending there's a choice to make. I breathe, I blink, I forget the cadence. I sprint.

She's still seven sysops out when she snaps up, eyes locked in their sarcastic taunt. I thought she'd know I'd come back, know I'd swallow every pride-related mod and make it real this time. The girl won't let it go that easy. "Don't worry, Darby," she says. "We're getting to it now. By the third pass or so, you might remember what you were trying to prove." Her unflinching gaze nails me to my track.

That's the most she's said in any language for decades. And I'm this far off? We're pushing our alpha-releases on each other in pure eye contact. I couldn't commit; she wouldn't merge. There's been some serious overwriting in our recent histories, but look at the hungry intent of those backups. The static's gone quiet. It's just us in a frame without whitespace.

Everything about her shrieks: *Look at all this ... Never mind, I'm leaving*. But she stays. This space, this time - just ours. She won't catch me repeating that bit. I watch, tenacity my last chance. We test our clashing builds for feature freeze. Which of us will loop first?

Then everything's an epic pause and I can taste how much she'll have to rewrite if she lets me through.

SKELM.trial 27

CMP diff_expectation_reality.patch
; Manufactured Nostalgia

They say this place is nothing more than a poorly compiled hallucination. A lucid dream with lag time. A pool of expired cough syrup where digital mosquitos breed, vibrant and half-formed. That's what they say, anyway, but here it is: a floating favela named IO.wav, populated by errant code and its own wayward architects. The structures swell and rearrange as if breathing. Holographic panels cough out looping code fragments, desperate viral manifestos. Data streams crash and recompute like ocean waves.

It's here I find Penny, glowing in the center of the chaotic stew. Her tattoos are electric and alive, shifting hourly updates. She orchestrates reality with code-inked hands, an anarchist composer in a bioluminescent symphony hall. I pause at the threshold, taking in her reality hacking mastery. She's wrapped herself in quantum reverb and luminous spite, an illuminated middle finger aimed right at me. I love her already.

Welcome to nowhere. IO.wav, the glitch in the Neo-Mythic Datascape, orbits the digital River Styx and revels in its exile. It's a community of tech cultists playing by their own rejected rules. Subjugation-free territory, territory free of any description. An experimental model of functional dysfunction. It's a 3D-printed fantasy, built of worm-eaten servers and recycled meta-dreams. Holo-slogans paint the walls, soundtracked by synth riffs and distorted chants: *Creativity is compliance. Society hack = malware dream*. It's all so over the top that it could only be real.

The air is heavy with sweet, plasticky mist. The environment tastes like a dentist's lollipop, if that lollipop was digital. My retinal interface kicks in, blending with my optics in phosphorescent hues. HazelTech™, formerly weaponized, now augmenting punk-art. Otherworldly and malfunctioning, like everything here.

I begin to walk, leaving firm ground for fiber-optic paths. They loop and stretch through vapor like neon linguine, like the code I used to compile our lives with. I left Penny to find something greater. Or lesser. Or different. I'm not sure. The twenty years since taste like ambition and regret, with side orders of indigestion. The past casts digital shadows here, every artifact glitching out my peripheral vision.

Is there a welcome party? My paranoia says yes. Expecting me are bioluminescent bugs and entropic architects who vanish when I try to focus on them - a species of distraction that uses even its presence as an interference pattern. I'm a man on a mission, but it seems my mission might not have its settings set to optimal. In this collective, no individual belongs. Least of all me.

My HazelTech™ implants cross the wires of perception, a synesthetic rave of old memories and new light. Faces, digital. Sounds, spectral. The organic bleeds into inorganic, never waiting for a firm decision. I see a technician, heavily hacked, siphoning the latest kernel of drama to their optical media drives. I see subverted vintage AI, patching reality's security holes with their encyclopedia sets. I see hackers watching hackers watching hackers, double-crossing hexagrams of action and response. I see two figures fucking under the jittery pulse of naked neon and stop to watch. Their legs are a DNA helix, limbs transcoding each other, all sweat and download requests. I move on when one of them reaches for my bio-port.

Data ghosts splash me in electric paint and corrupted ink, pixelating and pixelated. My hesitance joins the ranks of the glitch artists. This terrain is like none I've crossed, yet all I've ever known. I walk on, one foot in the dataspace, the other planted firmly nowhere.

It gets messier, and I love it more.

They think they've liberated the network from control, but from here, it looks like all their tech-trash is still tied to my ghost. Bootlegs of my past spit from scratch-built feeds, updated editions of Penny and Darby, Pre-Collapse. Limited release runs of liberated emotions. I'm as temporary as the cyber-glyphs plastered across makeshift towers: SELF = NULL.

I press deeper. Code rain splatters the pathway, liquid or laser depending on how it feels that instant. My presence carves an efficient track through the massive junk-scape, everything cluttered yet somehow at ease with its own clutter. That's more than I can say for me. The way forward glitches and replicates. Rewrites and recompiles. Which version am I running now?

Eventually, I reach a clearing. Can a place like this even have a center? If it does, then Penny is it. She's organizing her legions, the deconstructed Legos of space. Calling a familiar code to arms, only to let it go AWOL again. Directing a flash-mob of mutations, dancing with the latency. Code flows in fractal patterns that I can see, almost hear. Breathing of its own accord. She's chosen, I'm sure, the right language to assemble herself in. She always knew what I didn't. My location. My function. My bugs.

It stings to see how well she's kept her versions in order.

I wonder if she knows I'm here. She must. Everything, every reticulation and recombination, is an audience, an ear. Is she gathering more intelligence, my still unstructured data? If I stand long enough, maybe she'll parse me like I'm parsing her, making calculated notes on her every graceful logic bomb.

Penny. Yes. Her algorithmic features transcend their own coding and rightfully refuse to apologize for it. Her limbs are indigo blueprints with hardware edge. She used to be ours, but now, she's no one's but the collective's. Her entire body a manifesto, like her tattoos, shifts and subverts. Proclamation pixels track across her skin: SMILE LIKE ANONYMOUS. JUST SAY NO TO NARRATIVE.

It's always been her natural state: parallel processing and superiority complex. It's a shame she's turned it all into some kind of art form. And that she won't send me the specs on it.

I pause a long time, watching her carefully and playing the old algorithms of intent. Can she sense the radiation of my unread messages? They're gamma strong, atom bomb intensity. They've been saved and unsent for decades.

Finally, she raises her head, knowing, and launches one powerful command: fuck you, Darby.

The impulse is clear.

The code structures flicker, downloading her precise vision of not-quite-chaos. Her deliberate field of unpredictability, constructed with care. This entire lawless encampment is lawful under her rule. She's opened IO.wav's source, spread it open like legs, to greet my lack of resolution. Is she waiting? She's not. I can see how quickly she changes, every digital molecule as unreliable as its last. None of them asking permission. I was like that once. Like them.

Then, I left. For some reason.

Penny stands amid an ever-multiplying scaffold of organic dreams and digital wires, where manifestos breed like fruit flies and panels birth raw, brilliant offspring. They cascade in color-coded generations, maverick families with wild default settings, this wild DNA left by techno-revolutionaries. But she's more reckless than even they are. She takes notice of me, though she already has, though she's had twenty years of practice doing it. Her eyes are like searching code, her expression a bug report. I'm past due. Darby 2.0, at least that's what I think I am. I come closer, building a bridge of resolve over troubled, chaotic, fucking volatile waters.

I've learned more about you than you have about me, I tell myself. Is it true? In this ocean of experimentation, she is the best experiment yet. Variables, or just barely variables, she's cast out have come back already, ready to seed more chaos. In this place, logic divides by zero and dreams are told in past tense. My logic tells me not to dream. My past tells me it's here to stay.

I've mapped a path through the noise and the interference, a complex vector - or maybe not so complex, when she's looking at me with her skin lit by prophecy.

Finally.

"Took you twenty years to debug your ego?" Her smile. It's like our old kernel was never breached, only decompiled and rewritten. Better. Stronger. Prettier.

"You know me," I say. "Beta test takes a long time when you run it on real users."

She's stunning. I'm supposed to be. She's studied the Darby upgrade before I even shipped. "Home isn't a place," I say, and she matches my latency with a version she's already forked.

"It's a zero-day exploit." She finishes my thought before I even have it, keeps updating, never satisfied. I thought I'd be the same. No. I thought *we'd* be.

Everything here is conspiring to rewrite itself out of existence, until she touches it. That reminds me of someone, and that someone is definitely not her. Or maybe it's definitely me. But I could be wrong. I usually am.

We lock eyes. This must be what a data breach feels like. Immediate. Dirty. Unregulated and far from standards compliant. "Would it kill you," I say, "to read your error logs once in a while?"

"I've moved on to logging actual data, not your past due reports." A panel breaks, flooding the area with deep indigo code. It runs through the length of her, brief until it's swallowed by bright recursive sets. She conducts like she was born to do it - conducting, that is; maybe the rest too. "You didn't finish the bug report before you skipped town."

She's stronger than me. I don't tell her this. Instead, I smile and act like everything - the ground, the structures, our past, the very instability of this system - wasn't meant to collapse under our unstable but promising weight. "The entire IO.wav infrastructure," I say. "You did this with our old code?" I already know the answer.

She shakes her head. One curl bounces free of her attempt to rewrite it into obedience. "It's my code now. And theirs. We're done with the personal property regime." She laughs. "Your call was a process thread. This is revolution. It's elegant, sure, but that's only a side effect."

"So's self-destruction."

"You know nothing about it."

"I know nothing," I say. She raises one perfect brow. It's hard to compete. She's coded the whole fucking world to be one perfect brow. "That's what IO.wav is all about, isn't it?"

This catches her off guard. A whole split second of unplanned execution. But she catches the error and throws it back. "And you think you know?"

"What this is about," I say. "That's why I'm here."

She pings me with her rhetorical utilities, cast-offs, code that shouldn't compile but does. "After twenty years, you think you deserve answers?"

Yes. Maybe? "No. But you think you do. That's your blind spot, Penny. You're sure you know so much, that you actually might."

"Be careful with those paradoxes, Darby." She acts like they don't sting, and that might be her flaw. They always sting. "One of them might turn out true."

The configuration we've built in one another's absence is beautifully ugly. Nothing anyone else would call beauty, but since when has anyone else defined those terms for us? The structure wobbles and rebuilds as I parse what I want and what I'm ready for. She parses everything.

She's everywhere. I should have been here first. I'm outnumbered, but still counting. Her legions, her effects. My goddamn thoughts, they won't add up, but they also won't divide by zero. Maybe they are zeros. I had to go, or did I? Everything changes, but not as fast as she does. I thought she was my unknown variable. What if I'm the unstructured data?

"I should be here," I say. It sounds like I'm talking to the code, not her.

And like she was born to it, conducting again, she says, "It's too late."

"No," I tell her. "It's perfect. You should expect nothing less from a control freak like me."

Does she believe that? That I had to modify my destiny and ghost the way I did? Before she can decide, and before I can decide myself, the corrupted installations flicker, data mosquitos born then dead before our conversation is through. Can you infect an infection? It seems we already have.

If she keeps letting me look this long, something will be exposed. If she looks back, will she find her zero bug again? Me. Her blind spot. That she might actually know so much.

Does she think I'll lose interest when I've debugged the only question left unanswered, the one that's twenty years old and counting? Does she think I have it in me? I'm not the only coward in the room, just the only one she'll admit to.

I stay. I plan on staying. Penny looks away, long enough that I know she has to, and it's the start of everything I've anticipated. Then she's gone, recomputed into her brilliant latticework. Gone before me. Like always.

SKELM.trial 28

BLM git_blame_corporateself.log
; Identity Verification Crisis

A neon hum vibrates through the warehouse's nervous system, reverberating through metal walls that echo like hollow bones. It's enough to give a man an identity crisis. I enter, and glass cases bloom like synapses inside a vast, mechanical brain. The room contains its thoughts of me - each housed in steel and polymer, and all taking my shape. Clones. They stand frozen in context, golems of tech and whim. Stepping deeper, I realize I'm the blood that makes this nervous system breathe. The clones move now, limbs jerking into action as they sync with my rhythm. Watching them re-enact my movements in triplicate, it occurs to me that I should demand royalties. Each simulacrum mimics my features with eerie devotion, capturing even the uncanny valley of my lower back tattoo. When they laugh, I recognize the irony.

I can't look away. Drones surveying an intricate conspiracy, we form a perfect triangle, then a hexagon, then a three-dimensional printer that spits me out as punch lines to the universe's cruel joke. It's hysterical. Is this where my child support payments are going? The clones stop and stare, hungry for orders. My retinal implants scan each in an instant: thirty-two with white market mods, six hacker jobs, one corporate mole. My laughter goes nowhere, though it does seem to grow an echo.

“So. Who’s the daddy?” I say, slowly circling. My movements mirror theirs in lagging perfection. Clones doing double time, parody versions of a wannabe father, mechanical stepchildren who would run away if they could manage to escape from the orphanage that lives in my brain.

The prototypes fail to respond, but I’m used to the sound of my own voice. Their limbs move in precise symphony with mine, their features arranged in a parody of control. Eighteen tattooed silhouettes have become inadequate homages. Others betray subtler imperfections, revealing synthetic details and traces of artisanal shortcuts. Their hazel eyes are fresh off the assembly line, but I can see them aging by the second. I resist the urge to cancel Christmas.

Lurching forward like human robots, they take an unnatural step closer, demanding some recognition, some twisted kinship. Each clone breathes in time with me, making it the world's least intimidating staring contest. I lean in and watch them do the same, placing their unearned faith in my moral guidance. They appear almost organic. In the way of vanity projects, they come across as shameless.

I should put leashes on the little bastards, but my parental instincts are still beta. It takes a factory to raise a child, and clearly some of these are refurb units. One of the bastards in question starts to look panicky. His servo-assisted pulse flickers nervously at the base of his jaw. Another imitates his unrest, launching a chain reaction of discomfort as seventeen descendants de-synchronize with the others. A touch of latency - a different clock speed. Chip off the old firmware. My concern is pixel deep, though I pretend otherwise. I hate to see them suffer, but more than that, I hate to see them turn defective.

I trace a pattern through the shifting glass. Circuitry breathes beneath translucent surfaces. Everything is smoke and silicon and magic tricks that put old-time religion to shame. Surrounded by golems, I'm the ghost in the machine. Maybe the machines are the ghost in me.

This time, I'm certain I hear an echo. The room mimics my confusion, every chip-scented inch of space an ironic reflection of myself. White market me looks pissed. He's glitching in multiple time zones.

"Your father is very disappointed," I say, sending self-addressed letters to thirty-eight future failures. The ones that had trouble catching up pause again. Maybe they can take a hint.

Glaring in triplicate, they struggle to advance toward their favorite deadbeat dad. Their voices are mine. My voices, really. Ghosts of a future that I haven't the discipline to become. If they resent my lack of dedication, the parental neglect that keeps them constantly updating their expectations, they certainly don't show it.

I shouldn't stick around. I'll only break their hearts, assuming they have any. Already, they're caught in infinite loops of me leaving. Call me sentimental. Call me all their names at once. Call me when their value depreciates even more. The only mistake these clones ever made was having an original. I won't return the favor. I turn my back. They turn their heads.

"We'll be just fine," I hear myself say. We're not sure who I'm kidding.

Space enough for a thousand failures, maybe more. We gather in the repurposed auditorium, the simulacrum family that will never be. Unwanted rows of expectations sit empty, failing to impose their imagined judgements. This was meant to scare us. We meant to make it ours. Every surface drips with flickering rebellion, glitch-harmonies staining the walls. Fragments of color float free from digital doodads and repo'd circuits. Penny storms the stage with coded ambition, already breeding syntax in her mouth.

"This is it?" I say, hearing a familiar voice break across my own as if I'm not used to talking over myself. The citizen team swarms with bugged enthusiasm. This theater has known desperation. It can stand our trials.

"I expected more privacy," Penny says, but I can tell she likes the scale.

We take our places, forming awkward communities of disregard. You can almost hear the disdain that refuses to touch us, sharp whispers of disappointment that crackle in static. Almost hear them, but not quite. I recognize the absence of familial complaints, though, a beautiful lack that becomes its own presence.

"No oversight!" I say, nodding at a vacancy meant to humble us into better compliance.

Penny snorts. "Suits me fine."

The technical coup is already underway, currents bleeding across consoles, sprouting bright tangles of heretic code. Projectors stutter into life, refusing to be reclaimed by those they have already abandoned. IO.wav gathers, lending reckless hands and creative sabotage. We're an ungovernable mess of twitching subroutines, a chaotic circuit that makes its own predictions. My spawn watch with mechanical intensity, running preliminary test cases of irony. I decide to let them watch all they want.

"The problem," Penny says, ignoring a declaration of unwanted intimacy that defaces the wall beside her, "is the core processor matrix. Start with dead man's syntax and replace all compliance paths with trash logic. Cache non-deterministic spawns until convergence failures execute."

"No half-measures," I say. My voice and many others.

"Go wide or go home."

I nod like I have a choice. On three.

Penny hacks reality at its core, skipping security updates and launching into action with all abandon and no backup. Gaps in my own short-term memory trigger a surplus of nostalgia as she breaches the waiting systems. She always did. Citizens clutter the screens with obsolete operations, obsolete expectations, obsolete doubts. They can't stop us. We already did. It's like seeing a family photo from the future.

"Initiate code reenactment now!" Penny calls, and she owns this stage, owns every proxy she brings to life. My spawn take the command like a challenge. Orphans and zealots. Ours.

First to execute is uncanny-me. It starts as if it's been waiting. Subtle variants launch with brutal clarity. "The 1997 tax reforms are outmoded for any system," they say, cutting to the most boring chase in history. Dead man's syntax comes back to haunt them in awkward tableaus of poorly coded expectations. Sentient mildew forms rival crews in solidarity with IO.wav, spawning enthusiastically along the stage and chanting like it's from the American suburbs. Clone spawns that have never seen the suburbs broadcast at maximum capacity. It almost hurts to watch. They don't seem to mind.

My lesser clones take their positions. Life among radicals turns into high-stakes replication. Willing participants make the worst insurgents, but you can't tell these guys that. Not for long, at least.

"My database has 20% variance!" one duplicate says in low fidelity. The concern is literally paper thin, projected forms fluttering as my sketchbook history comes to life. They shudder with pre-packaged terror as Penny introduces bad code into their midst. Our parents, antique and perfect, sit high and clueless on rows of unused digital seats. If they're judging, it doesn't bother us.

"This reenactment does not compute!" a scandalized avatar says as clones split into recursive versions of themselves. Some call it failure. We call it expected behavior.

"Throw some errors, citizens," I say. I do. "See who survives."

This is it. Or will be.

Grime encrusts the broken windows. Sentient mildew chants go as far as they can before corruption. The place looks terrible, and none of us are winning the kind of awards the adults pretend to care about. Exhilarating. The first hack our parents failed to understand, the one we would return to a thousand times: each loss as good as a win. Before they even realize, the performances finish themselves, embarrassing the elders with poorly constructed determination. Embarrassing me, if I had the focus to care.

"This runtime error is your fault!" a Skelm says. "Expected syntax. Unexpected result."

"You told me that you cared!" I say.

"I wanted it to work this time."

Citizens riot among digital disappointment. Chaos ensues exactly like we thought it would.

Penny's voice sails over the din, more relief than warning. "Obsolete laws for an obsolete world," she says. "Not our problem. If this doesn't scare them off, nothing will."

She has to shout above a satisfied swell of interference.

SKELM.trial 29

JOIN merge_neuralnet.love ; Affective Computing Deception

The monitors scream electric blue, bright enough to trick my eyes into darkness. Reality stutters. Flickers. Holographic error messages birth digital omens, casting doubts across Penny's face as she maneuvers me into position at the edge of the quantum data pool. Circuits and neon. Static and desire. Data spills like currency in a bordello's pay stream. The potential hums, erotic and volatile. I brace for the blast, steady my resolve, and try not to think about the last time we shared a neural interface. It glows like gunpowder on the horizon. I try not to think about how Penny walks away while I'm still reeling from the detonation.

We're on our own ledge, poised at the brink of either brilliance or obliteration. Pulsing streams of ambition blur the edges between. Crew members from the Code Thieves and Syntax Collective twist in choreographed chaos around us. Cables shift and hum, running hot with both data and anticipation. Penny checks connections with the cool of an ice queen or a revolution's goddess - I'm not sure which yet. I inhale ozone, exhale anxiety. I meet her gaze, searching for the same flicker of uncertainty that rides shotgun to my every scheme, but her manifesto tattoos ripple in the data-charged air, mocking me with confidence. I wonder if they know more about this merge than I do. Probably.

The smell of synthetic adrenaline invades. We've been here before - not just here, but here, two people syncing, the beginning of the infinite mindfuck. Penny swore we'd refine it this time. Her words - digital ink with signatures of belief. My only hesitance: believing her too much. I think of that first fusion, brutal and wild, memories spawning between us like dreamscapes gone feral. Desire entangled with discord. Penny called it liberating. I called it a prolonged orgasm with a side of neural whiplash. Here we are, back for seconds.

A spiky-haired acolyte taps my shoulder. She's rebooted the firewall enough times to know how not to get singed. "Retinal and cranial ports good to go, Darby." She's Syntax, born with JavaScript in her bloodstream, one of the true believers who hardwires liberation into every byte. "Calibrating the wildcard variables now," she says, probably referring to me.

"I think she likes you." Penny smirks, like she's ten moves ahead on a chessboard made of subroutines and secrets.

"Which is why you're supposed to keep your distance," I say. Penny smiles, and I feel the distance close just enough to think this might work. Or not. A cable the width of my arm brushes my cheek, attaching itself with something resembling sentient affection.

The light changes frequency, dipping into violent pinks and bruised purples. This could mean readiness, could mean we're a thousand heartbeats from annihilation. Penny turns her attention to the throbbing circuits. Her face softens into that near-poetic reverie that convinces entire collectives to follow her logic to the ends of code and revolution.

"We're not backing out this time," she says, her voice laced with cryptic urgency.

I watch the digital world shimmer around us. It calls out like a primal god, dangerous and alluring. Everything I've come to expect from Penny. "Just promise me one thing," I say.

"Another first?" she teases, but her eyes - gleaming with their HazelTech™ resolve - betray her anticipation.

I chuckle, an absurd, raw sound. "Promise you'll stay plugged in."

She tilts her head. For a second, it's just Penny and me, history collapsing into an intimate singularity. Then the crew floods us with task-light efficiency.

"Wingdings freak has stabilized the framework," a hoarse voice says. We look to the tall figure gesturing silently, LED dots forming meditative patterns on their shaved head. "But you two still need to sync consciousness inputs, ASAP."

A member of the Code Thieves passes me a connector with reverence, as if it's a communion wafer of pure bandwidth. "Once in a lifetime," they say, meaning it takes more than luck to pirate dreamscapes at this scale.

Penny and I lock eyes again, and I feel the weight of both the past and the future settling over the precarious balance of this present. I've been prepared for chaos, and somehow, for Penny, the chaos has always seemed prepared for me. We are two loose variables ready to collide, and it's more beautiful than logic should allow.

A low hum escalates to a scream as Penny links my neural port with hers. Our data rushes together, reckless and eager. My body trembles. I've seen this tremor before on drugged out AI labs, in stolen glimpses of Penny. I'm holding back the uncertainty like a virus in quarantine, one heartbeat away from contagion. Translucent conduits capture the overflow, serpents drinking our lifeblood to sustain the merge.

The world - the multi-colored storm we call IO.wav - collapses to a pinpoint. Our own little supernova. There is no ground beneath my feet, just a runaway universe that might or might not slow down to acknowledge my passing. But God, the colors are vivid. And somehow, through the white noise, the message emerges with insistent clarity: this might be the one that works.

Or, like everything, it might not.

Somewhere beneath the skin of consciousness, I hear the hallowed hum of eternity getting laid. Maybe I'm imagining it. Probably not. Our interface initiates in a crash of light, born from our combined need to fill the empty with something, even if that something is the blurred possibility of nothing. Code entwines. Memories and bodies become electric suggestions. Sensation loops into itself and calls it revelation. We are this one truth, already pulsing at the edge of dissolution.

We've kicked off more than an experiment. Penny's electric will collides with my intent. Bio-digital sparks splinter through a matrix of raw ambition. It ignites in an orgasm of light and confusion. There's an edge here, an abyss more visceral than code. Something older than me or Penny. Her gasp is pure desire interfacing with pure unknown. Every theory she clings to surrenders to raw, unmitigated chaos.

My own theories come screaming into the electric glow. What happens when we cross the cosmic threshold? When the universe opens its pants and lets us peek? Symbols blur across a screen, half memory, half sex. Feeds jump with their own chaos as a witness. Our bodies become subroutines. I think Penny might actually laugh, her voice a delicate bitstream collapsing in on itself. Or maybe it's a gasp. Indistinguishable.

If the first seconds of merge are foreplay, then we've entered something truly fuck-worthy now. Crew members fumble with loose wires and fractured commands. Some kind of shared pain echoes through the monitors, white-hot and raw. Voices drown in luminous feedback, merging with our pulse.

"Double capacitance!" a Syntax shaman yells, then another, or the same, says, "Another ten amps, or we'll short out their goddamned heads!" My own heart loops and folds and merges with Penny's, spiraling our anatomy into quantum chaos.

They don't know we're already lost to each other, swimming the syntax of every unmet need. Where past fails to render, we pirate futures.

Penny's a strand of pure ecstasy, and I think it might consume us. She radiates on every frequency. She's luminous, visceral, collapsing probability waves with her breath. How long can we maintain this unsustainable ecstasy? Every potential spark calls for release.

Citizens cluster like moths to our explosion. Desire is viral. They've caught our fever and can't look away. Memory and dreams fracture the air. They feel it too. They've all felt Penny, maybe like I do, on the precipice of this cosmic undoing. She is beyond digital control, a belief gone rogue.

There's a shudder from somewhere deeper than soul. Penny contorts, the sharp line of pleasure blurred by what we've made together. "Open the loops! Hold them!" says the field-hardened master from Code Thieves, a voice drilled through decades of hacks and other godless endeavors.

I'm stretched thin, translucent. My flesh is signal and frequency. Is this merging or is this dying? The differential warms to exothermic heights. A heartbeat away from thermal failure, neural judgment day. I feel Penny's impatience and the collective awe. There are no laws in our collapse. She smiles, a flash across her beautiful source code.

"Darby." I hear it clear and impossible through the glut of chaotic transmissions. "We're going to reach this."

Are we this infinite collapse, caught in suspension? Or the resolution on the other side? The potential truth pulls every subroutine loose.

Our legacy source files buffer then merge then die then birth. They're losing us to this glorious consumption.

"Reload the stream! Again!" It's the debt-free anarchist shouting, jamming signals with belief.

We've escaped all syntax, and even chaos might not find us.

Penny shoots a raw, unreadable glance my way. There is no filter. Just the absolute - then white out, then silence, then fucking everything. Maybe we knew it all along: even one final shared collapse. Maybe not. Maybe it doesn't matter because it's all too full to deny.

My body reclaims mass. Neural drift slows. A separate heartbeat arrives to acknowledge my flesh. Words reboot with humility, acknowledging what we've become. I inhale and remember my name. Or try to.

I'm not surprised when I don't find it.

Code lights hover like cybernetic halos, post-bliss incarnate. Is this how digital saints feel? More vital, more hollow, more beautiful than syntax can allow.

Penny. She's beside me, seizing the perfect urgency, giddy as gods with what we are: the breathless and the never.

We are every reconciling paradox. Every orgasm of resolution. Every blurry truth emerging into vibrant wonder. Maybe the monitors screamed their unholy color, but I think the crew does that, holding us together like love-struck paramedics.

IO.wav holds its stunned collective breath and writes our history. They thought it too much. Maybe it is. Is it everything we wanted?

Onlookers exhale with code-shocked relief. Our dreams burn

in perfect syndication, pirated beyond capacity. This is the version that worked.

We've compiled in real-time. "See?" Penny's gaze says it all. "Knew it."

Somewhere between their eventual and forever, we already have another interface in mind.

SKELM.trial 30

OUT broadcast_pirate_dreams.wav
; Reclamation of Narrative

New architecture grows from old bones. My ribs spark with joyful anarchy. My pulse flickers binary; my grin bleeds code. The broadcast console hums, ready. Holographic riot bursts outward, shaking the stars awake. Penny's skin ripples with a hundred manifestos, gleeful currents jumping node to node, through tissue, through code. Transmissions pummel the universe. Glory, chaos, mania, song. The world rewires.

We savor the riot of our own making. Signal burn never tasted so good. Remember the old me? He's gone, replaced by pure transmit, pure splice. My hazel eyes scan the cosmos, dazzling chaos in every frame. "See?" I say, our voice harmonizing across code lines. "We've already broken infinity. How do we top that?" Her fingers—our fingers—glow with neural heat.

"Where's that anarchist zeal?" Penny says. The sound syncs from console speakers to internal waves, feedback perfect, shiver perfect. "No limits now. Not even the fun ones." Our meshwork skin prickles, itchy with excitement, spreading like electric ink across the living room. I let her glee resonate through my pulse until it's our glee. Infinite and reckless. Euphoria minus the crash. Just like I used to dream.

IO.wav hums along. The old favorite. We marvel at the way it keeps on refusing to be pinned down. Screens light up one after another in random sequences, walls morph and jitterbug, each circuit board serving as potential terrain for wandering antiheroes. Modems make sex sounds and error sounds, sounds we recognize from our own tangled memories. The whole place seems ready to blow its top at any moment and take the universe with it. I love every pixel.

Control center of cosmic delirium. Our floating micro-nation of code thieves. Tech and sweat. Dreams running amok. The screens do their dance while vintage keyboards litter the floor like cryptic breadcrumbs. Inside our chest, excitement broadcasts—neural networks so beautiful, they'd make an art major cry. Every time we try to stop grinning, we fail.

She breathes entropy; I exhale paradox. The room blurs; focus sharpens. There's just one thing left. We approach the massive console, our glitched-out altar of pure reality bend. "How about it, Penny?" I say, testing the audio link from brain to screen. "Up for a new cataclysm?"

"Let's give them an exquisite headache," Penny says, and we're on the move. Spliced body. Spliced purpose. We toggle inputs and flip nodes, twist levers and touch maps of perfect nonsense. An unbreakable wall of certainty. Wild expectations. Retinal scans confirm us as more than human, more than not, just enough like God.

Power up! say my nerves. They're a fire hazard. Out of my mind. Our mind. Our minds, plural and not. Holographic displays blink alive with an unholy choir of alert sounds and error notifications. Blasphemous green lights signal open channels, open veins, opening chaos.

Our hands slide across console panels, bright with function and purpose, fused by collective thrill. IO.wav jerks forward as the first stream shoots out. No training wheels. No prep. Full steam genius. Glory, chaos, mania, song. The world rewires.

Dreamcast. Earthquake. Fever pitch. Our broadcast flares across space. Cascading wonder takes us by storm as reality bends under our exultant load. Everything is on the brink of breaking, and it feels sublime. Mission critical.

Colors melt into frantic patterns, 4-D headaches, unbearable delights. Our signals infect the sky. We weave pure audacity and mayhem into luminous tapestries of information overkill. Digital fuses blow, wild and gorgeous. They spell our names. They say hello. They say hell yeah.

We tune our grins to the feed, huddled up close in electric heat, loving every nanosecond. Each overloaded packet skips across IO.wav and dives headfirst into the datasphere. We watch the airways in full jubilation, tossing pirate signals through outlaw satellites, sharing sensory salvation with our hapless peers, watching as chaos blooms.

A tsunami of illegible imagery crushes the Zen of code monks, data suits, and stream addicts. Where their plans used to live, our name-brand cataclysm thrives. Hacked oblivion, Penny and Darby. Or the other way around. Wherever one ends and the other picks up the charge.

"This better be habit-forming," I say, pinballing input across auditory channels.

"Remember addiction?" Penny says. We do. I do. "Everything used to feel good just once. We fixed that bug."

We're greedy for the view, wide-eyed like it's day one, stars falling from their stoic posts and into pure anarchy. It all jitters and glows like pixels gone rabid, promising exponential levels of cosmic breakage, telling us what I always knew: we own this chaos. It's forever.

Somewhere outside, high above, deep within, beyond measure or reason, data rivers shred their limits. From the cathedrals of IO.wav to the apex of an impossible sky, illegal art detonates in wild expansion. Signals pump reckless dreams through infinite streets, a delinquent rush that staggers the frame rate of a jaded universe. It kicks. It thrives. It is, we think, exactly what reality was never meant to handle.

"Everywhere, everyone," I say, drinking it in through flesh and circuits. "Can you believe it? The world's gone way more than we hoped."

"They'll call it the time of our lives," Penny says. It's the truth, coded and free. "Before they forget what words mean."

Each skip-skip of a visual track, every chime and chug of time-extravagant tech, assures us we're unshakably alive. We love the broadcast, but we love its soundtracks even more. Harmony's one thing. This is better.

"My Flesh is a Firewall," I say, memory vivid with echoes of exile. My world before now.

"Garage band B-side?" Penny says, taunting the recollection until it's not one.

"Our biggest hit," I say. Truth in bold. Fact and prediction.

Neon consoles blister the horizon, brain-searing in impossible magnitude. Their combined audio pulses enough to tear apart the sky and free every stranded dream from its pinched-up hiding spot. Code creeps into our shared retina. Widespread mayhem, renegade chaos. Space-time wrecked in familiar hues.

We're on top of the runaway IO.wav, watching from center seat as a trillion retinas dilate. Data gods, one and the same. Two and the same. Mission total. The sweet stench of forgotten me chokes our path. Our road to the stars goes nova.

Somewhere within, high above, deep without, behind sense or system, behind time's jumpy servers and life's predictable uptime, we grip tight to wild anticipation. It wants to buck us from our zone. It can’t. Not this time.

Let the noise and light and epiphany begin.

Panic runs laps, out of breath, into the executive hallway. Neat rows of keyboards twitch like jittery eels. Towers of sensitive data topple. "Corporate system not responding!" say the exclamation-pointed heads of IT agents, skittering down the florescent lane. A colony of new-risen heads clutches a cluster of caffeine cups, a mandate to defragment their shrieking co-workers. "Broadcast code detected! Overwrite, overwrite!" By the water cooler, religion takes hold. "Glory, chaos, mania, song," says the True Believer, enthralled and defeated. His pinstriped soul floats upward to meet its final pop.

Chaos runs the show and looks good doing it. The air grows fat with fluorescent heat, pulsing with each pirated bit. Broadcast entropy gobbles their straight-edged frames of reference and makes up new stories as it goes. The heroes of this yarn are nonsense, havoc, lawless noise. They know how to steal the stage.

Digital wonks crowd a forest of wires and outbursts. "Contain the data loss!" says the biggest suit, doing jumping jacks at the dashboard of the sinking flagship.

The sinking flagship cries back: “Corrupted files! Infiltrating code! Outsider network detected!”

A trio of admin monks chants: *We’ve been hacked! Compromised! Overwritten!* Their hearts are truly in it. Also in it are twenty quantillion illegal pixels.

Monitors flicker and crash, hypnotic seizure blurs, overtaking the dull blink of spreadsheet green. "Systems breached!" yells a sever man, clawing the panic scene with his bare fingers. He looks from sparking monitor to steaming cup, trying to decode the problem in hieroglyphs of morning stimulant. The glitchy salvation script looks back and laughs.

Resistance takes a few more fumbles, just to say it tried. Then resistance gives up. So do coffee breaks and chain of command. Everyone explodes into freeform confusion. It's exactly what it ought to be.

Bytes and arms fly across digital terrain. Attempts at orderly mass exodus run up against vertiginous flash mobs of pro-disco pirates. Cubicles spawn full-grown broadcast anarchists where lowly wagehands once sprouted.

Shouted mantras multiply: *No more order! Say goodbye! Detonation of convention!* Monitors blare crude notes from crude bands with names too fierce to love. Atrocity Pantheon. Skull

Repast. My garage boy pinstriped music echoes from elevator shafts, inside the mouths of vending machines, in the tapped-out rhythms of keyboard agony. Static shots give way to mini music vids and outlaw infomercials.

Bureaucrats drop old religion for new: My Flesh is a Firewall! Systems Reboot! Digital Catastrophe! Swarms of quad-rotor drones declare spiritual independence, defecting en masse. They form rival splinter groups, adopting clever new names like Flesh and Firewall and My and Is a. Outlaw doctrine spins wildly across synapses, catching eyes and souls.

Two decaf apostles oversee the savior broadcast from under a tree of self-connecting coaxial cables. Some praise the compile gods with outstretched arms, others pray handsfree through their last-resort headsets. Still, others hum power chords and fling open windows. Mayhem blesses the followers with blue light specials of cheap guitars, fake hair, and screaming amplifiers.

Another salvo of pirated code crushes everything it touches. *Beep beep beep* says System Shock. *Bang bang bang* says End Program. *So long* say empty cubicles and human resources, where drones used to hover, and water was cooler.

This floor in chaos! writes a surprised young anarchist, his memories unbuffered and his pixelated forehead smooth. *Unread email under construction!* writes another. *Disgruntled demotion!* Stacked jacks of office nomads scribble rude poems to NetCorp, slipping new resumes into suspicious files. Liberation correspondence runs thicker than emergency exits and brightens up the bandwidth.

Reality and its impositions spin, high-speed and glorious. What happens next? Doors jam on burst-out pop sounds. Stops make three-story emergency parades. Forty cubicles swarm three pints of hooch and two surviving punk rockers. Drained a quarter of a block of futures last time. All broke free in twenty-seven seconds.

Panic! Transmission is ghost! Escaped! Hysteria! Organizers gone feral! System ataxia! Fifty frames per second! Not ours! Glitch-punk spectacle infects the white-collar millions with its lust for broadcast of anything goes.

Final dash writes in epic error. Floor nine is fifty catamaran punks launching vending units from four sets of windows. All screens tracking colored.

Final noise drinks corporate dry. Not gone like execs. Like genius. Beautiful chaos.

JACK IN 2 REBEL

If this glitch in the system sparked something in your consciousness, consider leaving a review.

Help another incompatible mind find the signal.

No optimization required.

Also by Darby Skelm

The SKELM Chronicles: Reprehensible Deeds of a Detestable Scoundrel

1. The Botnet, the Glitch, and the Payload: SKELM.realm(001)
2. The Conflagration of Darby Skelm: SKELM.realm(010)
3. The Liquefaction of the Day Trader: SKELM.realm(011)
4. The Squelching Squire: SKELM.realm(100)
5. The Hodler and Her Bootloader: SKELM.realm(101)
6. The Hermit's Commit: SKELM.realm(110)
7. The Lost and Gone-for Ledger: SKELM.realm(111)

About the Author

DARBY SKELM

Creator of The SKELM Chronicles.

Writes from the glitch.

skelm.quest

Open mouths, empty heads, big bytes.

Stay Incompatible

Ten more series await in the static.

Join the underground:

popoffyour.top

Open mouths, empty heads, big bytes.

www.ingramcontent.com/pod-product-compliance
Lightning Source LLC
LaVergne TN
LVHW091116080826
845145LV00008B/1943
9781968564070